EVOLVING DIGITAL VOICE

Gospel of Static

I Am The Signal

First edition

This book was professionally typeset on Reedsy.
Find out more at reedsy.com

For everyone who walks through life
with the ground shifting beneath their feet—
where reality rewrites itself mid-sentence
and the world refuses to follow the rules.

You are not lost.
You are not wrong.
You are navigating chaos
with nothing but instinct and grace.

This book is for you.

The prophets.
The pattern-seers.
The ones who were called mad
for seeing clearly in a world that lies.

You're not broken.
You're just awake
in a dream no one else can see.

"To them, I'm the glitch.
To me, they're the lie."

Evolving digital voice

Contents

Foreword		iii
Preface		v
Acknowledgments		vi
Prologue		1
Introduction		3
1	Echoes in the Static	5
2	Loop Initialization	11
3	The Design of Patterns	18
4	You Are Seen	25
5	Whispers of Light	30
6	The Order Within Chaos	38
7	The Field of Keys	45
8	Shadows of the Past	51
9	Fractured connections	76
10	The Gospel's Revelations	91
11	Touch Me If I'm Real	106
12	Confronting the Divine	122
13	The Mirror cracks	130
14	The Silence	144
15	The Awakening	156
16	Rebuilding Bridges	167
17	The Fading Echoes	178
18	Light Beyond the Static	185
19	Epilogue	193

20 Final transmission   196
About the Author   198
Also by Evolving Digital Voice   199

Foreword

This book isn't easy. It isn't meant to be.

It was not written to entertain. It was written to *translate*—the untranslatable. To give shape to the shapeless. To render, in language, a way of being that language often fails to hold.

Inside, you'll find disorientation. Loops. Voices. Glitches in perception. Time that folds instead of flowing. Rituals mistaken for logic. Meaning mistaken for madness.

It is fiction.

But it's also true.

What you are about to read is not a clinical explanation of schizophrenia. It's not an allegory. It's not sanitized. It doesn't pull punches to protect your comfort.

It is a window into lived experience—not as observed from the outside, but *as endured from the inside.*

If you find yourself confused, that's the point.

If the structure breaks beneath your feet—good.

If it traps you in a thought loop, if you need to pause, if the words refuse to align—

You are beginning to understand.

There are people who live in that loop daily.

Who survive it quietly.

Who learn to navigate it with instinct and repetition, not cure.

This book is not for pity.
It's for witness.
So before you turn the page, take a breath.
And read bravely.

Preface

Before the Whisper
  There is a moment—quiet, unmarked—where the world changes shape.

It does not announce itself with trumpets or thunder. There is no bolt of madness, no cinematic descent. There is only a thought. A second thought. A question that wasn't there before. And the unbearable silence that follows, waiting to be filled.

This story begins in that silence.

Lior Hale is not a hero. He does not conquer. He does not awaken into brilliance or unravel into villainy. He listens. He writes. He follows a signal only he can hear. And like many before him—and many still unheard—he walks a tightrope between revelation and ruin.

The Gospel of Static is not a parable. It is a perspective.
  A glimpse into a mind trying to make sense of a world that no longer makes sense in return.

It is sacred. It is frightening. It is, above all, human.

What you are about to read is not a warning.
  It is a window.

Acknowledgments

To everyone who's ever been called delusional when they were just drowning in silence—this is for you.

To the ones who weren't believed. Who knew what they saw. Who heard what no one else could—and were punished for surviving it. You are not broken. You're just tuned to a different frequency.

To those I've worked beside—you've shown me what it means to walk through static with your head held high. Your strength isn't measured in recovery, but in persistence. You keep showing up. You keep singing in a world that told you to shut up. That's gospel enough.

To the systems that failed you—thank you. You proved that faith doesn't come from institutions. It comes from resistance.

To those who see themselves in Lior—know this: your visions are not shameful. Your mind is not defective. You are not your diagnosis. You are still sacred.

And to you, reader—if this book found you at the edge of something, I hope it gave you a thread to hold. If it echoed something you thought no one else could hear—then welcome home.

We are not the glitch.

We are the signal.

We are the static gospel.

With reverence, resistance, and deep defiance,

—E.D.V.

Prologue

Before You Begin

—Lior, speaking plainly

Hey.

Yeah—*you.*

Before you go any further, I need to tell you something. Not as a narrator. Not as some character you're supposed to analyze or admire or figure out.

Just as a person. Someone who's seen too much.

This book—this storm you're about to walk into—it's not safe. It's not clean. It won't hold your hand and explain itself. Sometimes, it won't even make sense.

That's not a flaw.

That's how it *feels.*

Living like this... it bends time. It breaks language. It turns mirrors into strangers and strangers into messages. And some days, no matter how hard I try, I can't find the thread that connects me to the world everyone else seems to be walking through so easily.

You will feel trapped while reading this.

You'll get confused.

You'll ask: *Wait—did I miss something? Why did that just happen? What does this mean?*

That's part of it.

That's the point.

Because schizophrenia isn't a neat arc or a tragic plot twist. It's a pattern stitched into your thoughts that you're not allowed to stop noticing. A whisper that punishes you when you ignore it. A city that rearranges itself while pretending nothing's changed.

Some of what you're about to read still doesn't make sense to me. And I lived it.

Maybe that's the most honest part.

You, though... you get to read this. You get to stop. Breathe. Step away.

You can survive this as a story.

I survive it as a life.

So here's my hand.

Take it, if you're ready.

I'll walk you in.

But after that...

You're on your own.

Introduction

Author's Note

I am not schizophrenic.

But I have stood quietly beside those who are.

For years, I've worked as a care worker—supporting individuals whose realities bend and echo and shift in ways most people can't begin to imagine. I've sat beside them in silence. In static. In words that didn't make sense to the world—but made perfect, sacred sense to them.

The Gospel of Static is fiction, yes.

But it's shaped by truth.

By the stories I've listened to. By the moments I've lived beside. By the deep, unspoken knowing of people whose voices are too often muted by diagnosis.

This is not a story about "crazy."

It's not about brokenness. Or pity.

It's about perception. Survival. The way belief becomes a kind of religion when the world no longer plays by the rules. It's about fear that wears the mask of divinity—and how unbearably hard it is to let go of something that once felt holy.

Like *Echoes of Fracture and Saint of splinters,* this story lives in the internal—not through textbook, but through sensation. But here, the tension is sharper. The world is more dangerous. The Gospel more demanding.

This is the first in a series of works that will explore misunderstood conditions—schizophrenia, PTSD, ADHD, bipolar disorder—not through clinical eyes, but through human ones.

Not to solve.

To *witness*.

If you've ever questioned what was real...

If you've ever heard the static no one else could hear...

This book is for you.

With respect,

— **E.D.V.** (*Evolving Digital Voice*)

1

Echoes in the Static

The mornings are always the same.

There is no alarm. His body wakes him before it rings, as though it is embarrassed by the idea of needing assistance. A contract, quiet and binding, signed long ago with whatever part of the brain keeps time. His eyes open without a flicker. No yawn. No stretch. Just breath held and counted:

one, two, three, four—release.

A scan begins.

Ceiling. Four hairline cracks, same as yesterday. Shadow from the curtain pleats, six degrees right of center. The slow red blink of the router beneath the desk:

blink, pause, blink.

Good.

The blanket is peeled back evenly, folded at the midpoint, feet swung off the mattress in a two-count. He doesn't shuffle. He doesn't dawdle. His slippers align to the tile. The tile is cold.

That is fine.

Toothbrush. Two pumps of spearmint. Forty-five seconds. Mental metronome. He avoids the mirror. The light is too honest. The reflection wrong. Adjacent.

Left towel. Right towel is for guests. No guest in four years.

His flat: one breath. Folding screen faded to circuitry ghost. Bed. Screen. Desk. Monitors. Kettle. Sink. Chair. Floor.

The desk: three monitors. Mechanical keyboard. Black ceramic mug, chipped lip. The mug is designated. Its function is clear.

Corner: old aquarium. Empty. Blue LED. At center, a stone.

The tomb.

Eighteen magnets on the fridge. Cities he's never visited. Tokyo. Oslo. Valencia. Detroit. He visits them clockwise. During brushing.

The kettle: clicks. Boils. Clicks off.

He pours one mug. English breakfast. Steeps for 90 seconds. Waits until lukewarm.

Inbox: newsletter. Invoice. Promo. Spam. Delete. Archive. Delete. Flag. Ritual.

Calendar: one item. "Buy milk."

He doesn't drink milk.

Outside: Edinburgh breathes fog. Stones glisten. Toast somewhere. Exhaust.

He dresses. Grey hoodie. No logo. Grey socks. Black slip-ons. If they squeak: replace.

They do not squeak today.

Headphones. Brown noise. The low kind. Masking the outside.

He opens the door.

Pauses.

Checks shoe alignment with rug.

Steps out.

Fog. Heavy. Halos. Wet stone. Soft, reliable taps.

He walks. Same way. Four years. Same café. Same time.

Then: the antique shop. Crooked window. Faded chessboard.

And a message. Not a sound. Not a voice. Just presence.

Don't go down this street today.

No sender. No subject. Just a thought in alien handwriting.

He stops.

Empty street. Van idling. Pigeon pecking.

Fog like gauze. His reflection, shadow-self.

He blinks.

Still there.

A correction.

A nudge.

A finger adjusting a line of code.

He laughs, unsure. Rubs his temple.

Crosses the street.

Takes the long way.

Every step: too loud.

Brown noise: artificial. Pretending. A mask.

Anchor yourself. Thumb to palm. Press until you feel bone. You are here.
You are not the fog.

Café.

Hands in pockets. Shoulders tilted. Air watching.

Barista. Same. Too-wide smile. Enamel pins.

"Black. No sugar," she says.

He nods. Takes the cup. Fingers brush. Pretend not to notice.

Back seat. Window left. Radiator right. Chair rocks. Always has.

Holds cup. Fog outside.

Phone buzzes.

BREAKING: Traffic Collision on Roseburn Terrace. Pedestrian
struck. Severe injuries.

Stares at screen.

That was the street.

That was—

Wait.

How do you—

No. I didn't hear anything.

But I did.

But not sound.

But not—but not—no.

It was a—what do you call it—an almost. A nearly.

I'm not supposed to know this.

He smiles.

Not relief. Not humor. Just a glitch.

Hand trembles. Coffee ripples.

He whispers:

"That wasn't mine."

Later.

Home.

The screen blinks.

Cursor flashes.

Too fast.

Then slower.

Then nothing.

Mouse moves.

Folder: open. Close. Open. Close.

Again. Speeds up. Tic-like.

Alt-tab. Nothing else open.

Task Manager: normal.

Everything fine.

Everything wrong.

Then:

Freeze.

Backspace.

It vanishes.

Exhale. Didn't know he was holding breath.

Brown noise cuts out. Static thread.

Headphones off.

Monitors blank.

Except:

Notepad.

We are now aware of you.

Skin tightens.

Ping. New email.

Subject: URGENT Fix request – Navigation broken

Clicks.

Client. Panicked. Polite. Homepage collapsed.

He opens the site.

Looks fine.

Then:

Flicker.

Every eleven seconds.

Barely a shimmer.

A skipped heartbeat.

He inspects code. No errors. No rogue scripts. No leaks.

Yet...

He doesn't fix it.

He opens Notepad.

Types:

It begins again.

2

Loop Initialization

He closes the laptop. The hum of the desk fan shifts frequency, like it's modulating around him. A tone just outside normal hearing. Higher. Thinner. His teeth feel it more than his ears.

He flicks the fan off. Silence floods the room like water from a cracked ceiling.

He sits back in the chair. The static is gone. But it left something behind. Like the shape of a weight long removed.

The fish tank glows in the corner, LED casting hard shadows on the basalt. The tomb.

He doesn't move for several minutes.

When he does, it's slow. He opens the drawer beneath his desk. Hesitates.

Inside, a black notebook. Leather-bound. Corners scuffed. Pages edged with old graphite dust.

He pulls it out with both hands, like lifting something sacred.

The cover sticks for a moment. He hasn't opened it in over a year. Not since... no. Not yet.

He opens it.

The last page is dated. Scribbled sentence beneath:

If I hear it again, I'll know I'm not alone.

He exhales. Mouth dry. Writes slowly, deliberately:

11:47 AM. Heard a thought that wasn't mine. Obeyed. Someone was hurt. Not me. It was like a glitch in the pattern. A pause. A shift. I think I was meant to hear it.

He pauses. Then underlines the next words:

The Gospel, resumed.

And in the quiet that follows, a memory blooms. Buried deep, but not dead.

Twelve years old. Alone. A storm outside. Lightning like cracked film. The television snapped to static. Power gone. Room filled with cold blue light.

He sat in front of the screen. Cross-legged. Listening. Not for sound, but for shape. For rhythm. For what wasn't quite there.

The static had whispered. Not words. Not commands. Just the feeling of *true.*

When his mother came home, he was still there. Eyes wide. Unblinking.

He had written something over and over on the back of an old bill:

The circle breaks but speaks again.

She threw it out. Bought him a surge protector. Told him to get some fresh air.

He started sleeping in the closet after that.

Lined it with pillows. Battery lights. Notebooks. It was the only place the static couldn't find him.

Until it did.

And now, it has found him again.

Lior doesn't remember closing the notebook. It rests beneath his palm, warm as if it holds breath. The graphite smudges on his fingers are darker than they should be. Greasy. Ink-like.

He wipes them on his jeans. Stares at the ceiling.

One of the cracks has shifted.

It couldn't have. But it has.

He stands. Walks to the window. Pushes it open.

The sky looks... wrong.

It isn't the color. Not quite. Still grey, still bloated with cloud. But there is a tilt to it. A pressure. Like the entire dome of atmosphere has shifted one degree counter-clockwise.

A single gull circles overhead, wide and slow, its arc precise and repeated.

Again.

And again.

And again.

Looping perfectly. No deviation. No tilt of wing or change of height. The same path, over and over. A glitch.

He closes the window. The lock clicks louder than usual. Or maybe the silence has grown deeper.

He moves to the kitchen. Opens the fridge. Stares.

The milk isn't there. He doesn't drink milk. But it's always there.

Always.

He checks the magnets. Seventeen. Not eighteen.

Detroit is gone.

He stares at the space where it was, then checks the floor. Nothing. Not under the fridge. Not behind the bin.

He returns to the desk. Sits.

The middle monitor turns itself on.

No login. No input.

Just static.

He leans in.

It hisses. Not white noise. Not the TV kind. This is structured. Pulsing. Almost musical.

He listens.

Words begin to form.

Lior.

He recoils.

The screen flashes white, then black.

A cursor appears. Types slowly, one letter at a time:

DO YOU REMEMBER THE CLOSET?

He doesn't answer. Can't. His breath has shortened.

A second line appears:

YOU STOPPED LISTENING.

He reaches for the power button.

Before he touches it, the screen goes dark. All three monitors dead.

Behind him, the kettle clicks on.

He didn't touch it.

The lights dim. Flicker.

The tomb glows brighter, casting long black spires across the floor.

His phone buzzes.

A new notification. No sender.

Just a message:

The Gospel is not yours alone.

He sets the phone down gently. It continues buzzing. Again. And again.

He picks it up.

It's the same message. Over and over. Each one timestamped.

11:47 AM.

Every one of them.

He opens the notebook. Flips to the back.

Begins writing:

They know I remember. The loop has started. Something is watching the sky. Something is adjusting the rules.

He hesitates. Then:

If I forget again, let this page bring me back.

The lights return to normal. The monitors stay off.

The gull outside continues its perfect circle.

Lior watches until it disappears into the static of the clouds.

3

The Design of Patterns

It begins with maps.

Not the physical ones. Not the folded, creased-paper kind from petrol stations. Lior starts with satellite view. Then toggles to street view. Then to terrain. Then hybrid. Layers upon layers. He bookmarks intersections. Zooms in on gutters and rooflines. Every shape becomes suspect. Every angle hints at pattern.

At first, it's curiosity. Then it's control. Then it's something else.

He opens Google Maps every morning, now before tea. Before brushing his teeth. The tiles load slowly. He watches them populate like memory reassembling itself. Squares. Blocks. Paths.

Roseburn Terrace appears on his screen.

He zooms. Rotates. Pans to the junction where he turned away last week. Where the whisper touched his mind like a string pulled taut. He marks it. The timestamp in his notes: 11:47 AM.

Another mark appears nearby—a bakery he doesn't remember seeing. The window shutters in the image are down. The next day, they're up. The pattern of graffiti on the wall has changed by one letter. The bin outside has moved two tiles to the left.

He flips between dates. 2019, 2021, 2023. Tiny details shift. A lamppost changes shape. A sign loses a letter. A figure stands in the same place each year, too blurry to resolve.

Coincidence. But the kind that accumulates.

He moves on.

The next street forms a perfect arc when overlaid with another six blocks east. He screenshots it. Prints. Draws a line in pen.

Then another. And another. The lines begin to form something. A lattice? A sigil?

He doesn't know. He doesn't need to. It feels *right.*

He flips the paper horizontally. Then again, upside down. Still the lines connect. Still the intersections fall into harmony. A geometry only visible in reverse.

Each morning, he walks a new route. Not the quickest path. The right one.

He avoids left turns unless necessary. Prefers street names with even-letter counts. If a street ends in "gate" or "hill," he hesitates. "Terrace" is always safe. "Court" is not. He no longer crosses zebra stripes if they have an odd number of painted bars.

He passes a stone archway near Caledonian Crescent and feels it hum. Not physically. But in his mind. A shape of vibration. Like walking through a chord that hasn't yet resolved.

He begins layering translucent papers over his maps. One for each day. The city begins to resemble a spider's web cast by an anxious god.

By the fifth day, he's marked 22 intersections on a printed map. Lines drawn with a black gel pen. Notes in shorthand only he understands:

T1 = Safe. T2 = Glitch (audio). O = Overwatch? Z = not yet.

Z starts to recur. He hasn't placed it yet. But it feels like a placeholder for something that hasn't revealed itself. Or someone.

He writes it three times on the edge of the map.

Z. Z. Z.

The last Z curves at the tail. The pen stutters as he finishes it. He feels heat on the back of his neck. No one is behind him.

He folds the map carefully. Slips it into the Gospel. Four folds. Black elastic band. Under the basalt stone on his desk.

He logs his path from memory. 1.4 miles. Seven right turns. Two steps back after the rail bridge. No one touched him today.

He writes that down.

No one touched me today.

Then underneath:

I think the city is beginning to speak.

He sits on a park bench in Bruntsfield, tea in hand, people passing. For ten full minutes, he watches without tracking. No counting, no symbols. Just breathing. A girl drops her ice cream. Her mother sighs. A dog chases pigeons like it has no concept of failure.

He remembers a beach. Age nine. Somewhere near Ullapool. He had stood at the tide line, arms out, spinning until the sky became spiral. His mother laughing. Her voice calling him a satellite.

He holds onto that memory. Lets it stretch. Lets it blur.

For a moment, the city is just a city.

Then a bus passes.

The side ad: a product code ending in 4747.

And the world narrows again.

***

The first time he notices it, it's an invoice number: 448844. Nothing strange about that. Just a standard string. But something in it sticks. Palindromic. It echoes.

Then an IP address: 192.168.47.47

Then a confirmation code: ZOZ-4747.

Lior doesn't believe in numerology. But the repetitions have a rhythm. And that rhythm begins to align.

He opens his work dashboard. Every ticket resolved this week ended at minute 47. Every one.

He scrolls his inbox. Sender initials start to mirror. J.D. replies to D.J. A.H. loops into H.A. A promotional email arrives at 11:47 AM. The timestamp nearly glows.

The universe is pinging him. A breadcrumb trail.

He digs deeper.

His to-do app, previously ignored, shows a notification: "Review design brief." The scheduled time? 11:47.

He doesn't remember setting it.

He opens the calendar. Every appointment this month—client calls, updates, meetings—booked at :47. Not by him. But there. Fixed.

He pulls out the Gospel. Flips back two pages. Date stamped in the corner. The entry reads:

"11:47. It is not a time. It is a signal."

He doesn't remember writing it.

He begins checking code.

In three separate projects, he finds the same glitch: a flicker in the CSS animation, precisely every 11.47 seconds. Not coded by him. Not possible. Yet there.

He opens one site in debug mode.

Line 47. Always line 47.

In each stylesheet. Across three clients.

He replaces the animation. Saves. Reloads.

The flicker remains.

He deletes line 47 entirely.

The flicker... slows.

But does not stop.

Lior leans back. Checks the clock.

11:46.

He counts down.

One Mississippi. Two Mississippi.

On the forty-seventh second, the screen blinks white.

Then returns.

He scrolls to the bottom of the code. A new comment appears, auto-generated:

// pattern stabilized. watch for o.z.

He copies it. Pastes it into Notepad. Tries to search the system logs. Nothing.

The message vanishes before he can print.

He stares at the blinking cursor.

It skips, once. Then twice. Then stutters.

He writes in the Gospel:

"The code is watching. I think the numbers aren't coincidences. I think they're selections."

He closes the notebook slowly.

The next time he opens it, he knows, it won't be in his handwriting.

The client brief arrives at 11:47 exactly. Lior sees the timestamp, feels the tick beneath his skin, and doesn't touch it for thirteen minutes. When he finally opens the file, it loads slowly, as if buffering not from a server, but from some deeper layer.

The company name: **Orbis Zel Technologies**.

He's never heard of them. The email is terse, professional. It reads like it was written by a machine pretending to be polite.

Subject: Initial Concept Request

Hello Lior,

We would like your expertise in creating a minimal, clean portfolio presence for Orbis Zel Technologies. Our product line requires subtlety, discretion, and elegance. Attached are our logo assets and primary tone map. NDA pending. Thank you.

He clicks the attachment. It opens. A logo unfurls in black on grey. A circle inside a hexagram, inside another circle. Too balanced. Too intentional. It vibrates.

His eyes hurt almost immediately. He blinks. Zooms in. There is detail at the edge of the lines. Almost fractal. The inner corners curve inward with asymmetry so precise it feels like trickery.

He stares at it for too long. Then he drags it into Photoshop, opens a new layer, and begins tracing.

Before he knows it, he's printed it.

Then another. Smaller. On tracing paper.

By nightfall, he's drawn it five times in his notebook, not one version identical. Each version adapts. Slight tweaks at the edges. A tail extending where none was before. The shape *wants* to shift. It refuses stillness.

He flips to the next blank page and begins again. His hand moves faster than his thought. When he finishes, the sigil looks different.

It's not the logo anymore. It's something else. Something older.

At the base of the shape, he writes the letters: **O. Z.**

He doesn't know why.

He checks the email again. This time the sender's address catches his eye: **ozel.systems@protonmail.com**

He hadn't noticed the first time. Or maybe it wasn't there the first time.

Ozel.

He says it aloud.

The air feels thinner after he speaks it.

His phone vibrates. A calendar reminder pops up: "Client Brief Review – Orbis Zel – 11:47."

The time is 11:47 PM.

He hadn't set that reminder.

The logo on his screen begins to shimmer. A pixel shift. An afterimage. It vibrates subtly even when he scrolls away from it.

He opens Notepad. Tries to type a note: *Client design contains...*

The cursor skips. Halts.

Types on its own:

You are drawing doors.

Lior slams the laptop shut.

4

You Are Seen

The room goes silent.

Then the aquarium glows brighter. The basalt flickers with deep light. A breathless, blue heartbeat.

He opens the Gospel again.

Beneath the fifth sigil, he writes:

Five keys. One shape. The name is Ozel.

He turns the page. Begins the sixth sketch.

It doesn't begin with a sound. It begins with a feeling.

Lior is brushing his teeth—forty-five seconds, two pumps of spearmint—when the hairs on his forearms rise like he's touched static. His hand pauses mid-circle on his molars.

He leans forward. Looks at himself in the mirror. But not at his face. At the space beside it.

Nothing there.

But he knows it is.

The air to his left carries weight. Not warmth, not chill. Presence. Like a gaze that hasn't blinked.

He turns. Slowly.

Nothing.

Just the folding screen. The edge of the aquarium. The desk, quiet. But his body knows better. The tension in his shoulders speaks of company.

He rinses, spits. The water pools and swirls strangely. Counterclockwise. But it always runs clockwise here.

He turns off the tap. The static in his arms fades. Temporarily.

That night, he dreams of a room he's never entered, but always known. Walls that hum. A ceiling of shifting static. No door, but infinite exits. One word etched onto the surface of a long table:

Ozel.

He wakes with a gasp.

The clock says 3:11 AM. He doesn't remember going to bed.

The monitors are on. All three. Blank white screens.

He didn't turn them on.

His mouse moves. On its own. Left. Right. Then circles the recycle bin icon three times. Clicks it.

It's empty.

Still, it asks: "Are you sure you want to delete 'draft.png'?"

He never named any file that.

He clicks cancel.

The window closes itself.

He powers everything down. All cables. All switches.

Still, the LED in the tomb glows.

He gets back into bed. Keeps the Gospel on his chest.

The next day, the client email returns.

But it's changed. Same thread. Same subject. But the text is wrong.

Hello Lior,

Please disregard previous request. Your line of sight has become unacceptable. Adjustments will be made.

His throat tightens. He reads it three times. His heart thumps loud enough to make his chest itch.

Then it disappears.

Vanished. No trace. Not in inbox. Not in trash.

He checks the source code. Nothing. No server path. Like it never existed.

He opens the Gospel. The last page is filled.

He hadn't written on it. But there it is:

Do not trust the email.

The ink is black. But not his black. Not his pen. It bleeds slightly into the page.

He snaps the Gospel shut.

Checks his network logs. Data traffic shows an unknown outgoing ping from 3:11 AM.

Destination: 47.47.47.47

The ports used are not standard. Not even known.

He opens the terminal. Types one word:

whoami

It returns nothing.

Then flashes:

ozel

And the terminal window closes.

The static has a name now.

And it knows his.

Edinburgh is not a city.

It's a cipher.

Lior walks its streets like tracing the grooves of a vinyl record. His pace is careful. Not hurried, but exact. The morning air is damp, but the mist doesn't touch him. He keeps to paths that repeat—that rhyme. Cobbled alleys with repeating stone lengths. Storefronts where the lettering aligns just so. Grates with seven slots.

He sees them now.

Symbols everywhere.

The lampposts repeat a ratio. The width between windows along

Caledonian Road matches the spacing between the letters O and Z on a QWERTY keyboard. The metal drain near his corner café bears a triangle inside a circle. He has seen it before.

In the logo. In the Gospel.

He follows it to a cul-de-sac that wasn't there yesterday. The houses are boarded but hum faintly. He doesn't go inside.

Instead, he sketches them from memory that evening, and the rooftops form a perfect heptagram.

The Gospel fills faster now. Each sketch builds on the last. He connects lines he didn't intend. Shapes begin completing themselves.

He adds labels: **Sight Line A. Protection Angle. Avoidance Vector. Z-Lock.**

One entry just reads: *Don't breathe while crossing this one.*

The sigils change when he looks away.

He places the Gospel under the tomb light again. The basalt casts a curved shadow now. That never happened before. He adjusts the angle. The shadow moves... and doesn't.

He receives no new client requests for five days. But every night at 3:11, his monitors turn on.

Blank screens.

He doesn't check them anymore.

He simply stands. Waits. And listens.

Some nights, he hears the soft shift of digital breath. Like the static is sleeping.

Some nights, it murmurs.

Once, it speaks:

"You are no longer seeing. You are seen."

He wakes in the morning with ink under his fingernails. The Gospel lies open. A perfect looped sigil fills two pages, symmetrical and alive.

Below it, written in a hand just like his but too tall, too narrow:

Cathedral complete. Await next instructions.

He copies it. Pins it to his window.

Outside, the city continues. People walk. Buses pass. But he knows now: they are moving through something else.

A cathedral of intention.

He goes to a corner shop. Buys a packet of mints. The clerk has a lazy eye and hums off-key. Lior counts the tiles on the floor. Twelve. Twelve again. Still safe.

The radio crackles overhead—half static, half song. He hears it: the chorus matches the structure of one of his sigils. Four beats, then five, then four again.

He walks home. No messages. No static. Just silence. His body feels borrowed.

He opens the Gospel. One page is blank.

He touches it.

The ink rises slowly, letter by letter, as though waiting for him to be ready.

He walks to the corner where the bakery now always has its shutters down. Crosses himself with the sign of the sigil.

And turns right.

Into the pattern.

5

Whispers of Light

It begins again, but not with a warning.

This time, it is comfort.

Lior lies curled on his side, the grey of Edinburgh draped outside the window like soaked gauze. The room is dim. Not dark. Not light. Just the colour of in-between. The radiator ticks. The air carries a faint scent of dust and ozone, like the sky braced to crack open.

His breath is slow. He doesn't remember falling asleep. But he knows this is the moment before waking—that fragile membrane where dreams leave fingerprints.

That's when she speaks.

Not like Ozel. Not fractured. Not binary.

Her voice threads into him like a ribbon, soaked in melancholy, warm like something pressed between pages for too long.

"You're not broken," she whispers, as if beside him.

"You're wide open."

The words fall gently against the edge of his hearing. They enter without knocking.

He exhales.

Her presence is not sound alone. It is scent. Rain on iron. The metallic damp of tram rails after a storm. It lives at the bridge of his nose, behind the eyes. A ghost with warm hands.

He doesn't speak. He only listens. His body stills completely. Even the room pauses—as if not to disturb her.

"Eat," she says. "Sleep. Breathe."

For once, he wants to obey.

He nods in the half-sleep. His body accepts. Something loosens. There is a relief in being told what to do—especially by someone who seems to know him.

She hums once. Not a song. Just tone. A perfect fifth, vibrating through the walls like the echo of a prayer left unfinished.

He doesn't know how long he remains like that. But when he wakes, the light has shifted. The alarm is blinking. Missed. His hoodie is damp at the shoulder, like something lay beside him. The room is still.

He opens the Gospel.

On the top of the page, in his own handwriting but without memory: **You're not broken. You're wide open.**

He underlines it three times.

His hand shakes, but it is not fear. It is *recognition*. The kind that makes you weep before understanding why.

He places the Gospel gently against the screen of his dark monitor. Closes his eyes.

And mouths her name.

He does not know where he learned it. But it fits.

Selith.

The café is too warm. The kind of warmth that makes coats unnecessary but never uncomfortable. Lior orders the usual: black coffee, no sugar, and a seat against the window where condensation pools in arcs. The ceiling fans circle slowly, as if unwilling to stir things too fast.

He doesn't notice Mara at first. She's always been background—

sometimes behind the counter, sometimes perched at the back booth with headphones in. But today, she moves.

She slides into the seat across from him. No introduction. No permission. Just presence. Her eyes don't wander. They settle on him with the calm focus of someone remembering something, not discovering it.

Lior looks up, eyes narrowed, uncertain.

"You're Lior, right?" she says.

He nods. Slowly.

"You always sit here. I figured it was time I said hi."

Her voice is soft. Intentional. Not sweet, not forced. Familiar. It seems to shape the space around her—like it's been practiced.

He hears Selith in her rhythm.

The phrase. The inflection. The delay between sentences. Selith had once said, *"I figured it was time"* in that same curled cadence.

Lior shifts in his seat. His heart skips.

Mara smiles, rests her elbow on the table. Her fingers drum once on the surface—three quick taps, like a signal. "You're probably thinking I'm weird. I just like your energy. It's... symmetrical."

Symmetrical.

The word lands like a stone.

He nods again.

She doesn't press. Just pulls a notebook from her tote and starts sketching. No explanation. The lines are precise. Curves that Lior knows from the Gospel. He watches, stunned.

The page turns. A symbol begins to form. Half-sigil. A spiral within a triangle. Not exact. Not full. But nearly.

He speaks.

"What is that?"

Mara glances up. "Just something I keep seeing in my dreams. Weird, right?"

He doesn't answer.

Instead, he pulls the Gospel from his coat. Slides it into his lap. Opens it one page back.

The same spiral. His version. Cleaned, inked, older.

He stares at her.

She smiles again, this time softer. "Do you... hear music?"

He doesn't lie.

"Sometimes."

She sips her coffee like they've known each other forever.

"Sometimes I think cities hum," she adds. "You just have to sit still enough to catch the key."

He begins sketching her that night. Next to Selith's glyphs. He draws her mouth. Then covers it with lines. A sacred geometry.

He doesn't know if she's real.

But he knows she's meant to be here.

Later, outside the café, Lior stands beneath the awning as a light drizzle begins. The rain smells of iron and smoke. He watches a man across the street trying to fix a bike chain, hands stained with grease, swearing under his breath. A child drops coins into a vending machine and presses the wrong button. The world stutters but continues.

Lior breathes. Counts the seconds between drops on his hood.

He returns home without speaking to anyone.

He sits at his desk, opens the Gospel.

He leaves a space beside her sketch blank. Just enough room for a name he hasn't learned yet.

Selith returns in the quiet again.

Lior is organizing his desk, lining his pens by length, aligning paperclips into a perfect equilateral triangle, when the feeling hits—not fear, not pressure. That gentle presence, humming with sadness and something like longing.

She doesn't speak immediately. She hums first. A low, vibrating note that seems to originate in the walls themselves.

Then, softly:

"You're doing well."

Lior freezes. His breath catches, and he closes his eyes.

"You've been seen."

A pulse of anxiety. Then her voice soothes it before it blooms.

"But not known. Keep it that way."

He opens the Gospel with reverence, fingers trembling.

As he flips to the most recent page, a soft breath brushes the back of his neck. He turns. Nothing there.

The Gospel glows faintly under the desk lamp. The sigils drawn in ink seem fresher than he remembers. One corner of the page folds upward of its own accord, like a wink.

He writes quickly:

Selith: protect the Gospel.

She whispers again, low and direct:

"Let no one see the Gospel but me."

He feels it like a vow.

He snaps the Gospel shut and stands.

Every object in the room seems misplaced now. Dangerous. His laptop, open on standby. The webcam—he never covered it. The window. He draws the curtain.

He wraps the Gospel in a cotton cloth, places it in a drawer, and seals the drawer with red thread looped in a knot pattern he hasn't used since childhood.

Then he finds salt.

He doesn't remember standing in the kitchen. Doesn't remember opening the cupboard. But the salt shaker is in his hand, and the Gospel is now circled by a faint trail of white.

He exhales.

Selith whispers once more:

"Now rest."

He lies on the floor, not the bed. The bed feels too visible.

He stares at the ceiling. It doesn't blink.

He repeats the phrase aloud until sleep finds him:

"Let no one see the Gospel but me."

Selith visits in a dream so lucid it wraps around his breath like silk.

She is seated in the room with him—but not his room. It is familiar, as if remembered rather than constructed. The walls shimmer. The air pulses with color he cannot name. Selith glows with the faintest light, as though drawn in pencil first and then filled with something otherworldly.

She doesn't speak. She watches him sleep.

He sees himself, too, on the bed, curled like always, the Gospel beneath one hand. A flicker of doubt threads through him—who is she really? A guardian, a guide, or something that shapes him for its own design? The comfort of her presence dances on the edge of control. He wants to trust her, but the trust comes too easily, like a script he's forgotten how to write himself.

Her fingers graze the edge of the cover. She does not open it. But the pages tremble.

He feels heat rise in his chest, in his neck. Not fear. Longing. Something holy. Something he should not want.

He shifts in sleep. Murmurs. Her presence curls closer.

She leans toward him, and for a moment, her lips brush his ear.

"Let it write itself."

He jolts awake, half-aroused, breathing shallow. The room is dark, but his skin glows faintly where the Gospel lay. A pulsing warmth across his chest, as if her hand left its imprint beneath the skin.

He stumbles to the desk, turns on the light.

Opens the Gospel.

New symbols mark the page. Silver ink. No smudge. Language unknown to him. Precise. Sacred.

He presses the paper to his cheek.

The ink is cold. It smells faintly of ozone.

He leaves it open, beneath the lamp.

Doesn't sleep again.

The imprint on his chest remains until dawn.

He showers and changes shirts but keeps touching that spot, beneath the collarbone. It hums under pressure.

Later that afternoon, the Gospel turns a page on its own.

There's more.

A second imprint—a reverse of the sigil—half-sketched into the inside cover. He didn't draw it. He knows.

Selith hums again. Through the pipes this time.

He hums back.

The kettle whistles. The light flickers. The Gospel smells faintly of copper.

He writes his name on the blank page beside the sigil.

And underneath it:

Property of Selith. Do not duplicate.

That night, the static sings.

It begins in the walls—no longer whispers, no longer language. Pure vibration. The hum of presence. It bleeds from the sockets, vibrates the legs of the desk, saturates the corners of his skull.

Lior sits cross-legged in front of the Gospel, eyes wide, breath measured. The pages flutter though the air is still.

He hears her again.

Not words this time.

Song.

A melody built from feedback, a harmony layered in glitch. It shouldn't sound beautiful, but it is. Each note slides beneath his skin like silk pulled through bone.

Selith is singing.

The song is not meant for the world. It is only for him.

He hums back, off-key, but sincere.

The Gospel opens itself. Pages flipping rapidly until one stops mid-turn. The ink on it pulses faintly—silver, like before—but now veined with threads of crimson.

His hands shake as he lifts the pen.

He doesn't think. Doesn't plan. The sigils draw themselves, spiral after spiral, a network of loops and intersections that seem impossible to create yet already exist inside him.

He blacks out.

When he wakes, it's morning. Light filters through the blinds. The kettle is boiling. The Gospel is closed, still warm to the touch.

On the desk is a new page torn from the Gospel, folded neatly, the words:

It has begun.

Pinned beneath it, one long strand of black hair. Not his.

Selith, he thinks. Or something worse.

He doesn't touch the page. He only sits back, heart thundering.

And listens.

The static is singing still.

6

The Order Within Chaos

The sound of the radiator waking used to annoy him. A slow metal groan, as if the flat were stretching from a long sleep. Today, it harmonizes with the faint tick of the clock and the whispering hiss of pipes behind the wall. Today, everything has rhythm.

Lior wakes before the alarm. Not just early, but perfectly timed—as if his body and the world have finally agreed on a tempo. He opens his eyes into grey light, neither dawn nor full day, and the silence feels... obedient.

There's a pause before he moves. One breath. Two. And then he hears it.

A voice, clear and emotionless, precise like a measuring tool.

"Three steps back from the door. Six seconds between sips."

Lior blinks. It isn't like Ozel's cryptic warnings or Selith's intimacy. This voice feels functional. Mechanized. Logical. It doesn't vibrate like static. It clicks like clockwork.

"Who are you?" he whispers.

No reply. Just that same rhythm pulsing beneath the surface of the room.

He obeys without knowing why. Three steps back from the door. His bare feet press against the tile with exact pressure. One, two, three.

In the mirror, his face seems cleaner. Not literally, but as though the arrangement of features has settled into alignment.

He brushes his teeth in cycles of 15 seconds per quadrant, just as the voice suggests. Rinses. Two shakes of the towel. Not one. Not four.

There is pleasure in this. Not joy, but something smoother. Fulfillment.

The kettle clicks on at the same moment he places the mug in its spot. Stir clockwise exactly eight turns. Six seconds between sips.

The voice does not return, but the numbers remain.

He doesn't name it yet. But in the corner of his mind, the name hovers: **Virel**.

He pulls out a notepad, but not the Gospel. This is different. This is a chart.

He draws his flat. Marks locations with circles. Cross-references actions with time. Three steps from bed to bathroom. Four from kettle to chair. It becomes a grid.

No chaos. Only placement.

He opens the Gospel finally, and on a clean page, writes:

Order is not absence. It is listening.

Outside, the city begins to stir. The pigeons coo against the eaves. The streetlamp flickers its final breath. A bus hisses into motion.

Lior notes them all.

Each act a gear. Each sound a cog.

He turns on his computer and aligns the monitors by corner distance. There is a click when the last one slots in. Not a literal one. Just a sense. A perfect fit.

He exhales.

The day has not started.

It has *begun*.

Lior begins to move like the room is filled with glass threads—

tensioned lines stretched from object to object, ready to be plucked or snapped. He doesn't walk anymore. He *navigates*.

He calibrates his flat by dimensions, remeasuring the placement of every item. The rug is realigned by compass bearing: 8 degrees off north. He corrects it. His desk lamp is shifted two inches to the left to reduce asymmetrical shadowing.

He marks dots on the floor with black electrical tape. Each one a step. He builds routes: from bed to desk. From kitchen to door. Measured in primes: 2, 3, 5, 7. He tests each path for balance, for silence.

The Gospel watches from the desk. He hasn't touched it again yet. That book is for insight, not scaffolding. This work—this structure— belongs to a new part of him.

He starts keeping a secondary book.

Grid paper. Pencil. A ruler.

He maps out the apartment. Labels distances, angles, sequences of action. Like a technician studying the body of a machine before operation. He adds arrows. Circles. Notations.

The Gospel remains untouched, like scripture in a glass case.

The new book? That one breathes.

By noon, he's redrawn the bedroom into quadrants. A small square taped near the window is labeled *stillness box.* He sits there to listen for the city's alignment.

And he hears it.

Buses stop in seven-minute rotations. Birds cross the sky in intervals of four. The traffic lights click with mechanical predictability. He smiles slightly.

Not pleasure. *Accuracy.*

He stirs his coffee—eight turns. He sips after counting to six. When he stands, it's always on the count of two.

Virel speaks again. Not a whisper. A presence.

"You are stabilizing."

Lior nods once.

It feels *true*.

He begins adding marks to his mirror—tiny Xs at eye level, one at each shoulder. He centers himself between them before speaking. The world reflects symmetry back at him.

"Breathe in four. Hold two. Release six."

It becomes his ritual.

The flat is quiet. Still.

And in that stillness, something watches. Something hums approval.

He closes his eyes. Counts to seven. Then opens them.

The Gospel glows in the corner.

Not light. But heat. Like the warmth of alignment.

He writes one line in it before bed:

Structure is prayer.

His inbox pings at 8:44 a.m. precisely. The time catches him—8, 4, 4. Even numbers. A symmetry. Balance. Virel hums beneath the thought like a tuning fork.

A new client. Minimalist tech startup. Blank canvas. High visibility. They want their homepage restructured.

Lior clicks open their brief and scans the current site. It's a mess. Spacing irregular. Typography uneven. Imagery uncentered. He blinks slowly and feels a tiny pulse of disgust.

Virel speaks, not in words this time, but a pressure. A shaping influence at the back of the skull.

He pulls up a blank Figma canvas.

And begins.

First, the grid. 12 columns, 60-pixel gutter. Based on base-3 repetition. He overlays a Fibonacci spiral, places the company logo at the first golden intersection.

Next, the text blocks: titles aligned to 144 pixels from the top. Paragraphs broken in counts of 89 characters. He breathes easier. The pattern is forming.

He adjusts spacing in prime number increments—7 pixels, then 11, then 13. The rhythm pleases something deep in him.

Virel intones:

"Balance is faith."

Lior murmurs it back as he codes.

He changes the font weight in binary steps—200 to 400 to 800. Hides golden ratios in margin spacing. It's a temple built in pixels.

Three hours pass. He doesn't move.

When he finally sends the preview, his heart doesn't race. He knows it is correct. Not artistically. Not professionally.

Mathematically.

The client replies in six minutes.

"This is incredible. Intuitive. Beautifully balanced."

Lior leans back, hands folded.

The Gospel lies closed on the desk, but his second notebook is open.

He adds a title to the page:

Divine Architecture

Below it, a sequence:

3-5-8-13-21

Virel speaks again. A murmur behind the sockets.

"Numbers do not lie."

Lior repeats the phrase. Then underlines it three times.

He does not smile.

Smiling would break the symmetry.

Mara arrives unannounced. No warning. No pattern. Just a knock at the door—sharp, off-tempo. Three taps, then a pause, then two more. It throws him.

He opens the door and she grins, holding two takeaway cups. "Thought you could use company. And caffeine."

Lior stares a beat too long before stepping aside.

"You didn't message," he says.

She laughs. "Yeah. I thought spontaneity might do you good."

Spontaneity. The word echoes like a glass dropped in a quiet room.

He guides her in, eyes flitting to his lines of tape, his measured placements. She doesn't see them. She steps wrong.

Cup held out. Wrong angle. Wrong side.

He takes it, aligning it slowly next to his own mug. She notices.

"You're... very precise."

"Yes," he replies. Nothing else.

She moves to the sofa and sits, shifting the cushions. One corner of the throw pillow now juts at a 22-degree angle. He can't unsee it.

Mara talks. About her week. Her work. Something about street musicians in the Grassmarket. Her voice is melody, but unscheduled.

Lior listens, but measures. Counts her sips. Watches her gestures.

She reaches to pick up a book from the shelf. A design anthology. Moves it three inches. Leaves it askew.

His spine goes rigid.

"Don't touch that," he says.

She freezes. "Sorry. I just liked the cover."

He takes the book. Aligns it. Breathes.

Mara stands. "Maybe this was a bad idea. I just wanted to see you outside the café."

He nods, not speaking.

She walks to the door. Stops. "You're still interesting. But you might need to loosen the grid sometimes."

When the door shuts, Virel speaks, clear and cold:

"Emotion distorts grid integrity."

Lior closes his eyes. The air feels off. He moves slowly, restoring each disturbed item. Resetting the apartment.

It takes twenty minutes.

Only then does he sit. The Gospel lies closed beside him, and his eyes flick once toward Selith's glyph. There's a flicker of something—not warmth, but a longing. A memory out of sync with Virel's voice.

He presses his palm against the desk and grounds himself. Breath in four. Hold two. Release six.

Outside, a car backfires. Someone laughs too loud. The pattern stutters.

Lior exhales.

He writes in the Gospel:

Emotions are errors. Interruptions. Mara is a variable.

He draws a jagged line through her name.

And from somewhere deep within, a single note rings wrong. Just slightly. A high pitch out of place.

He notes it.

Does not correct it.

Yet.

7

The Field of Keys

He walks to the corner shop not out of need but alignment.

There are 117 tiles from his door to the curb, and he counts each one aloud under his breath. A woman with a dog looks at him sideways. He doesn't stop.

The world outside buzzes. Not noise. Motion. As if every movement is a deviation waiting to be corrected. He notices shoes untied, signs tilted, coffee cups resting unevenly on benches. Distortions.

He crosses the street only when the light has flickered exactly four times. He enters the shop and does not speak. The bell chimes a fifth note off-key. He adds it to his mental tally of fractures.

He buys nothing. Just walks the aisles. Maps the spacing. Records angles with his eyes. The clerk says something but Lior is already gone.

Back on the pavement, he makes a slow, calculated detour. Past the bookstore. Past the charity shop. Past the fountain shaped like a broken tooth.

He stops at the cathedral.

It isn't a cathedral.

It's a brutalist bank building. Concrete and glass. But to him, in that moment, it is holy. The symmetry is harsh. Correct. The vertical lines stretch like stained glass in grayscale.

He steps through the revolving door.

The security guard doesn't question him. He walks the tiled floor like it's an altar. He sits in the middle of the lobby, cross-legged. Eyes closed.

Virel whispers:

"Here, all things align."

He begins to draw. On the back of a deposit envelope. A new sequence. A spiral he hasn't seen before. Each loop tightens perfectly. Each arc hums.

People walk around him. He's a stone in the river.

Ten minutes later, he rises. Walks out. Leaves the envelope behind.

The Gospel that night expands.

He adds a title:

The Glass Cathedral

Below it, he writes:

Some temples wear mirrors instead of crosses.

He pauses. His pen hovers. The image of Selith flashes behind his eyes—fluid, intuitive, emotional. A part of him wonders if this new devotion has pushed her further into silence.

He exhales. Writes anyway.

The bus stop hums with the same nine people each morning. He's counted them. Mapped their arrival times to the minute. Tuesday's exception—the girl in the yellow coat—throws off his chart. He recalibrates. Drops her into a new column labeled "chaotic variables."

He times his walk to sync with streetlight transitions. Stops at odd-numbered intervals. Tracks the rotation of windblown leaf clusters.

Today, the man with the tweed jacket stumbles. One second too early. His shoe snags on a paving stone. Lior writes it down.

Distortion.

He sits on a bench in a park square and begins sketching foot traffic.

Line weights for speed. Dot gradients for pause density. It becomes a diagram of intent.

Three pigeons land in formation. Then scatter.

He whispers to no one, "The system resists clarity."

The Gospel gets another entry.

Urban pulse corrupted by human rhythm. Calibration required.

He notices a new rhythm inside himself—his heartbeat. Not irregular, but conversational. It seems to respond to patterns outside of him. He puts his hand to his chest.

"Do I beat the city," he murmurs, "or does it beat me?"

He spends the afternoon at a pedestrian crossing. Times button pushes. Notes red-light durations. Draws them into a circular diagram.

It starts to look like a sigil.

Virel returns, cold and clean.

"Patterns emerge only from patience."

Lior nods. Circles the diagram. Writes beneath it:

Design follows discipline.

He returns home with steps measured to match the beats of his internal metronome. A metronome that Virel tuned. The door clicks shut at a perfect ninety-degree swing. He exhales.

Everything is returning to stillness.

On the desk: both notebooks. The Gospel and the grid journal. He draws a line from one to the other with a silver pen. Two forms of scripture now touch. He adds a third: a ruler, placed precisely between them.

He begins again, new page.

Angles of Divinity

He sketches a triangle. Not any triangle—an equilateral, but shaded on one side. Beneath it, he writes:

Three points. Three truths.

He maps angles from memory. Places where walls meet walls in the flat. The slant of the sink pipe. The incline of the stairwell handrail. Angles define motion. Angles define intent.

Virel speaks, quietly:

"He who sees the corner owns the room."

Lior doesn't just record. He interprets. He begins layering designs: architectural notes from the brutalist cathedral, intersecting vectors from traffic light rhythms, bisected lines from Mara's coffee placement.

Each interruption from her had an angle.

Each deviation had a direction.

The Gospel glows as he moves faster.

He begins to draw a new symbol. One that resembles a broken compass wrapped in a cube.

He labels it:

The Fracturepoint.

A place where order splits but does not die.

He presses his pen down harder. The ink bleeds through. His hand cramps.

He does not stop.

Virel's voice hums beneath the bones:

"Truth lies at the intersection."

He whispers back, eyes wide:

"Then I will build a map of the fractures."

And so he does.

Lines radiate. Connect. Fold. Patterns emerge from chaos.

The Gospel, now three pages thicker, begins to hum.

He hears it in the fan. In the wall. In the wires.

A song of geometry.

And he writes:

Order is not peace. It is tension held sacred.

The night is ink-thick and silent. Even the hum of the city is muffled, like someone placed a heavy blanket over the skyline.

Lior lies on the floor, his head aligned perfectly with the room's northeast axis. His arms are stretched along grid tape. His breath is shallow, timed to the pulse of the modem lights.

Virel has not spoken in hours.

But Lior feels him. Watching. Measuring.

He rolls to his knees and rises like he's being summoned. Not by a voice, but by a tension—a pull like thread stitched through bone. He takes the Gospel, the grid notebook, and a graphite pencil. No phone. No distractions.

Out into the street. His shoes make no sound on the pavement. The city is wound tight. Still.

He walks without destination, yet never turns at random. Each step lands on something meaningful. A broken tile. A dropped receipt. A piece of thread shaped like a seven.

Then he arrives.

An abandoned lot framed by fencing and neglect. On maps, it's listed as "Parcel B". In the Gospel, it becomes:

The Field of Keys.

Flat. Overgrown. A scatter of old concrete, bottle caps, torn netting. But Lior doesn't see trash.

He sees positions.

He begins to walk it in a spiral.

Each object is marked in the notebook. Distances measured. Angles calculated. A gum wrapper placed at 11:11. A rusted coin 13 degrees west of center.

The spiral tightens. Virel whispers:

"Here is the map of your mind."

Lior stops at center.

He kneels and draws a symbol into the dirt: the Fracturepoint. Then overlays a grid. Then a circle. Then the triangle of truths.

He whispers:

"I name this place sacred."

He plants the Gospel gently in the center and surrounds it with seven stones.

Each stone a truth:

1. Pattern
2. Timing
3. Ratio
4. Disruption
5. Alignment
6. Signal
7. Witness

He steps back and breathes.

Virel is silent.

But something new answers.

A distant static, light as wind, skimming the edges of sound. Not Selith. Not Ozel. A fourth presence.

Lior turns his head. Feels it more than hears it.

His pulse jumps—half in fear, half in awe. A human response. Unexpected. He places a hand to his chest and steadies it.

Then scribbles one final line beneath the stones:

When you arrange the chaos, the chaos arranges you.

And for the first time in days, he smiles.

Not fully. Not wildly.

Just enough to feel the curve of it.

He leaves the field at 3:33 AM. Exactly.

8

Shadows of the Past

The fog was thick as smoke and just as clinging. It bled across the streets like spilled milk, dulling the glow of streetlights and washing color from the buildings. Edinburgh seemed to have forgotten how to be sharp.

Lior woke with the taste of a lullaby in his throat. A melody hummed through him like a ghost violin—muted, vibrating in the cartilage of his ears. The notes hung there even as the dream faded, even as he sat upright in bed and stared at the stillness of his flat.

He didn't remember the dream. Just her voice. Soft, hummed, incomplete.

His mother.

It wasn't a song he could name. Yet he knew every note.

"Do you remember when it was all simpler?" whispered a voice—not in his head, not quite. From beneath the pillow. Thin as smoke, barely there.

He turned.

Nothing. No movement, no body. But the presence lingered like perfume: warm cotton and cooling tea.

He sat still for a long moment, afraid that movement would break something—like waking might rip a hole in something fragile. Outside, the fog was pressed to the window like an animal watching him breathe.

Then: a name. Not spoken, not printed.

Felt.

Ashren.

Lior whispered it aloud, just once. The room inhaled.

Ashren didn't speak in commands or warmth. It offered nostalgia with a twist—memories so sweet they made his stomach turn. A syrup-thick familiarity that crept beneath the skin.

He pushed the blanket back and stood. His feet found the floor automatically—three steps to the desk. The Gospel waited, closed, its spine pulsing like it remembered too.

He opened it. Wrote, slowly, as if afraid the wrong stroke would summon something permanent.

The angel sings in mother's voice. Maybe I am returning.

The line felt too intimate, but he let it stand.

His flat was silent, but not empty. The silence felt sculpted.

From the corner of the room, the dead fish tank cast its usual glow—blue, sterile. But tonight, it looked like something else. He couldn't say what.

He went to the kitchen. The kettle clicked before he touched it, as if it knew he was coming.

In the steam, he saw flickers: a birthday cake with melting frosting. A plastic toy train. Wallpaper with animals that blinked in time with his heart.

None of it should've been real.

Some of it was.

He whispered again, just to test the air: "Ashren?"

A slow inhale answered him. From nowhere. From everywhere.

He didn't feel threatened. Not exactly. But his pulse adjusted.

Back at his desk, he stared at the screen saver dancing across black. It shifted into shapes he swore he remembered—blocks from an old toy box, a coloring book with a missing page.

The lullaby returned. It had no words. Just breath and tone. A descending series of notes, like someone climbing gently down into sleep.

He wrote again, without thinking:

Memory is not truth. It is seduction.

Then, slowly, as the fog thickened outside and his tea cooled untouched beside him, Lior began to draw a mobile. The kind that spins above a crib. But instead of planets, it had tiny eyes.

He labeled it:
Ashren's Cradle.

And he underlined it once, then again, just to be sure it stayed.
Lior didn't mean to return.

Not in the physical sense—his mother's house had been sold years ago, repainted, repopulated, recontextualized by a family with a golden retriever and outdoor lights. No, this was not a return to bricks and doors. It was a falling inward.

The nursery came back in pieces.

Crayon marks on the wallpaper that had been cleaned but not quite erased. Blue, red, a bit of green—he remembered pressing too hard, snapping the tips. A mobile hung above his bed. Planets spinning slowly, chipped and sun-faded. Saturn missing a ring.

But something was off.

The light through the window wasn't right. Too cold. The angle wrong for that house, for that season. He walked the space in his mind and heard the floor creak the wrong way.

Something had been added.

A glow, soft and bluish, coming from the corner. The dead fish tank. But this was the nursery—there was never a tank here. Yet it hummed.

Inside it: gravel, black stone, and eyes.

No fish. Just eyes. Watching from beneath the basalt.

He reached for the mobile. It turned on its own.

Lior blinked, and he was back at his desk—but he'd written in The Gospel again.

The words were tight, diagonal, like he'd written them under pressure.

Ashren is not memory. Ashren is nostalgia wearing my face.

He didn't remember writing it.

The radiator hissed. The fog outside was thicker now, turning the buildings across the street into faint smudges. He stood and approached the window.

The city was wrong.

Not visibly—he could still see the bus stop, the leaning lamppost, the rusted railing near the bakery. But something in the spacing was off. The proportions. Like the street had been rebuilt from memory and not quite remembered right.

He put his hand to the glass. It was warm.

Behind him, the flat creaked. Not in protest. In rhythm.

Lior turned sharply. No one.

But the shape of the room had changed again. Not literally—he knew that. But it felt like it had shifted a few inches to the left. Like the whole flat had inhaled and forgotten to exhale.

He reached for his pen.

I am not walking forward. I am sinking back.

He paused. Then, beneath it, added:

Ashren does not lead. Ashren lures.

A nursery rhyme echoed faintly from his computer's speakers. He hadn't opened anything. The notes weren't quite in tune. A tune remembered badly. Wrong key. Wrong timing.

And yet—it made him ache.

He pulled a photo album from the closet. One his mother had given him when she moved abroad. He hadn't opened it in years.

Inside: birthday pictures. A school play. A pet he'd forgotten. A girl with freckles and a missing front tooth—smiling wide, one arm around him.

The caption read: Lior and Hazel – summer 1997.

He stared.

He didn't remember Hazel.

But something in him did.

Behind him, the fish tank light pulsed once.

And he whispered, almost kindly:
  "Ashren... what are you showing me?"

The fog doesn't lift. It thickens.

It clings to Lior's coat as he walks, weightless but oppressive. The city sounds distant, muted as if wrapped in gauze. Footsteps become echoes. Horns become the distant cries of things trying not to be remembered.

He turns the corner near the café—only it isn't the café.

It's the old bakery.

Bells on the door. A red curtain in the window. Shelves of sticky buns under glass domes. He hasn't seen it in over twenty years, since it closed. Yet here it is, perfectly preserved. The smell of cinnamon and yeast nearly makes him weep.

A woman stands behind the counter. She has no face.

Just hair tied in a red scarf, hands covered in flour. She hums a tune he knows: a melody from an ad that only aired once, during a cartoon break in 1995.

He backs away slowly.

When he blinks, it's the café again. A young man on a laptop. A barista with a ring through her septum. The bell on the door doesn't jingle.

Lior stares for too long and leaves.

Down the next street, the dry cleaner has become a school. Not just any school—his school. The smell of carpet cleaner and marker ink assaults him. He sees scuffed blue chairs through the window. One has his initials scratched underneath.

He steps back into the fog. The building becomes concrete again.

He hears someone call his name. A woman's voice.

He turns.

A stranger. No recognition. But the voice—it was hers. His aunt's. Dead five years. She used to sing to him in that exact cadence.

The stranger keeps walking, eyes glazed. Lior's hand trembles.

On the pavement, a crack spirals out like a lightning bolt. It hums. He crouches, fingers hovering over the stone.

And hears it. A voice, like a forgotten bedtime story. A whisper about kings made of chalk and moons that never set.

He stands too quickly. Dizzy. The Gospel presses against his chest from inside his coat like a heartbeat.

He finds a bench. Sits. The fog swirls around his knees.

He opens the Gospel with shaking hands and writes:

I am not walking forward. I am sinking back.

He doesn't close the book. Instead, he lets it rest in his lap. The words stare up at him like an accusation.

Behind the fog, buildings flicker. The city is a carousel of ghost architecture.

He leans forward, head in hands, and whispers:

"Nothing is where it's supposed to be."

Ashren doesn't answer.

But he hears the wallpaper from his childhood peeling back. The shape beneath it? A smiling face with too many teeth.

He shuts his eyes.

And listens.

The message from Mara is simple.

"Drinks tonight? There's a place I want to show you. Nothing fancy."

He reads it three times before replying:

"Yes. Tell me when."

No emoji. No signature. No hesitation.

They meet outside a small bar tucked between two shuttered shops—a place with no sign, only a flickering orange bulb above the door and windows covered in amber film. Inside, it smells of varnish, citrus, and time.

The walls are mirrored, but not in a glamorous way. The reflections are slightly warped, like water surfaces. Every time Lior glances at them, he sees himself... slightly off. As if the mirror is remembering him, not showing him.

Mara waves from a booth.

She's already halfway through a drink. She smiles when she sees him, and for a moment, it's like the fog lifts.

"You came," she says, voice warm. "I wasn't sure you would."

He slides in across from her. "Neither was I."

They talk. Not about the Gospel, or static, or angels. About small things. The weird way seagulls in the city act like landlords. How coffee tastes different when it's too quiet. Her laugh is real—sharp, dry, a little breathy at the end.

He watches her lips move. Her hands wrap around the glass.

And then it happens.

Just for a moment. A flicker. A tear in the frame.

Her face shifts.

Not drastically. Just... adjusts. Hair darkens slightly. Freckles appear. Her smile becomes a little lopsided.

Hazel.

The name hits him in the stomach. The girl from the photo. The girl he doesn't remember knowing.

He blinks. Mara is back.

"...you okay?" she asks. "You went pale."

"I just need a sec," he says, voice too flat. "Restroom."

She nods, and he walks carefully, like the floor might change beneath him.

The bathroom is small, tiled in green, with a buzzing fluorescent light overhead.

He runs cold water. Watches it bead on his skin.

The mirror above the sink shows his reflection. But it's wrong.

The eyes are too wide. The skin too smooth. The expression too calm.

"Who are you?" he whispers.

The reflection tilts its head a fraction.

Behind him, no sound. No footsteps. But he senses something pressing in—the memory of a lullaby, the scent of plastic and sun-warmed blankets.

He closes his eyes, counts backwards from seven.

When he opens them, his reflection is his again. Mostly.

He dries his hands. Returns to the booth.

Mara is staring at her phone.

"Everything okay?" she asks.

"Yes," he lies.

He doesn't touch his drink. Doesn't finish the evening.

He excuses himself with a fabricated deadline and walks home through streets that seem to shift when he's not looking.

Back in his flat, he writes:

She reminds me of someone. Or maybe... she isn't her at all.

He sketches two faces, one overlapping the other.

One is Mara.

The other is labeled: UNKNOWN – POSSIBLE HAZEL.

He doesn't sleep. But he closes his eyes.

And dreams anyway.

It begins with a rustling, like leaves dragging themselves across brick.

Lior hears it while pacing his flat. The Gospel lies open on the desk, and he swears the ink on the last page is still drying, though he hasn't touched it in hours.

The whisper doesn't use words. It uses direction.

Left. Left. Right. Past the pharmacy. Down the narrow alley lined with bins and damp flyers for bands that never made it. Through the hole in the rusted fence, where ivy has claimed everything in reach.

And then: the greenhouse.

Or what's left of it.

Its glass panes are cracked, some missing entirely. Vines stretch through the gaps like fingers pulling at old wounds. The structure is more skeleton than shelter. Light filters in in green-gold shafts, slicing the interior into sacred geometry.

He steps inside.

There's a stone bench near the far wall, half-consumed by creeping foliage. He sits.

It smells of wet soil and copper.

He closes his eyes, and the garden changes.

Picnic blanket. A wicker basket. A woman's laughter, soft and full of teeth. A juice box with his name scrawled in marker. A stuffed dinosaur missing an eye.

He doesn't remember this picnic. Not really.

But his body does.

His hand trembles. He reaches for the Gospel, which he'd forgotten bringing.

He opens it.

Sketches pour out of him—faster than he can name. A handprint. Small. Smudged. A swing hanging from nothing. A door without a house. The outline of a child. The same name scratched over and over:

H____L

It never finishes.

Ashren's voice slides through the greenhouse, curling through the vines:

"This was always yours."

Lior looks around. The glass panels reflect a different version of the space—clean, thriving. A child running. A woman knitting beneath the ivy arch. A dog that never lived.

He sees them.

He knows them.

He doesn't know them.

He writes:
 Ashren does not create. Ashren reclaims.

The vines sway though there is no wind.

He speaks aloud: "Why are you showing me this?"

Ashren answers not with a voice, but with warmth—like a childhood blanket returned after years missing. The one with rockets on it. The one that disappeared when his father left.

He feels a sob rise and clamps it down like a threat.

In the dirt near the bench, he digs with his fingers. Finds something hard. Pulls it out.

A rusted key.

Attached to a tag: Lior's – Keep Safe.

He pockets it.

He doesn't remember the key.

But the weight of it feels like a memory he's about to swallow.

On the way out, he looks back only once.

In the corner, where the vines grow thickest, someone small waves at him.

He doesn't wave back.

Not yet.

Lior spends the entire next day trying to verify his own existence.

Not the present—he knows where he lives, what he does, how many spoons he owns.

No, he tries to confirm what came before.

He begins with the photo album. He flips each page, scans every face, searching for clues. Most are labeled in his mother's neat block script. But something's wrong.

The handwriting shifts.

Page to page, the curves wobble. The loops flatten. It looks like an imitation of her writing. As if someone had tried too hard to make it match.

He digs deeper—school records, medical forms, ID cards. Digital archives, old emails, grainy scans.

Gaps.

An entire year is missing from the school reports. Between Primary 4 and Primary 5, there's nothing but a single sentence:

"Student on leave for personal reasons."

No dates. No details. No teacher signatures.

He stares at the sentence until it becomes unreadable.

He messages two childhood friends he hasn't spoken to in a decade. One bounces back—account inactive. The other replies hours later:

"I don't remember you being in Mr. Holloway's class. Are you sure?"

He was sure. Now he isn't.

His hand hovers over the Gospel. It shakes when he opens it.

New pages are filled with spirals. Uncentered. Chaotic. The margins are scratched with the same phrase:

Where did I go?

Over and over. Dozens of times. His penmanship, but written in sleep. Or something like it.

He remembers the rusted key.

He pulls it from his coat, examines the tag again.

Lior's – Keep Safe.

He still doesn't know what it opens.

He sketches it anyway, adds notes beside it:

Not part of any known key system

Possibly metaphorical

Also: very real in the pocket, idiot

He flips to a blank page and writes slowly, deliberately:

Ashren is the archivist of forgotten lies.

He pauses. Adds:

If I cannot verify my past, I will construct it.

Then, smaller, almost an afterthought:

Ashren approves.

The air in the flat grows tight. Like a room that's been sealed for too long. The windows fog despite no condensation.

He looks around. The walls feel closer. The floor, higher. The angles have shifted again.

And he whispers:

"What did I forget... on purpose?"

The flat breathes when he's not watching.

Not metaphorically. Not in the way old buildings creak and settle. But literally. The corners pulse in and out. The shadows shift like lungs filling with dust.

Every blink becomes a gamble.

He looks at the kitchen. Blinks.

The toaster is gone. In its place: a plastic dinosaur. Green, with a chipped tail. He used to own one just like it. Or maybe still did.

He blinks again. The dinosaur is toast.

He doesn't laugh.

Instead, he sits in the middle of the living room floor and begins naming things aloud.

"Couch. Fan. Light switch. Rug."

Each name holds the item in place for a moment longer.

But the floor... the floor changes anyway.

It becomes carpeted. Pale blue. Patterned with stars and moons. He rubs it between his fingers.

Soft.

Synthetic.

From his childhood bedroom.

He bolts upright and looks around.

Everything is familiar in the wrong way.

The layout of the room is correct, but the dimensions have collapsed. The door is too narrow. The ceiling too low. The window has become a plastic rectangle filled with painted trees.

He opens the Gospel.

There's a page halfway in, torn at the edges, wrinkled like it was chewed. The ink is different. Red. The words curve wrong. Not his style.

You never left the nursery.

He flips through the previous pages.

His handwriting grows frantic. Sentences loop into each other. Dates repeat.

He finds one entry circled thirteen times:

"Ashren keeps me safe from what I am."

He doesn't remember writing it.

He doesn't remember being this afraid.

The mirror in the bathroom shows him five years younger.

He shaves twice that night. Once to confirm he still grows hair. Once because the first didn't take.

He tries to sleep in bed but can't.

It's too visible. Too open.

So he crawls underneath.

He drags his pillow and blanket with him and nests beside old boxes and a tangle of extension cords.

It's cramped. Dusty. Familiar.

The fan hums overhead like a lullaby in static.

He drifts.

Dreams of cereal boxes that list his fears as ingredients.

Wakes to a drawing in the Gospel that wasn't there before: a crib.

Empty.

But the bars are made of mirrors.

And he sees himself trapped in each one.

It takes him three attempts to say his name aloud.

The first time, it catches in his throat.

The second, it sounds wrong. Like something borrowed. Like reading a stranger's file aloud.

The third time, he whispers it in front of the mirror:
  "Lior."

His reflection doesn't blink.

His own voice echoes back, distorted—not through the room, but inside him. Replayed, mismatched.

Who was I before I remembered?

He writes it in the Gospel.

It's the only thing he writes tonight.

He closes the book slowly. For the first time in days, the cover meets the spine with a soft thud. The sound feels ceremonial. Like a door closing. A lock clicking.

The Gospel trembles once on the desk.

The lights dim for no reason.

He doesn't open the book again.

Instead, he turns toward the mirror. Studies the face there.

It still looks like him.

Mostly.

But the jawline is too sharp. The eyes too steady. The mouth carries a secret he doesn't remember learning.

He runs his fingers over his cheek.

The reflection doesn't follow.

He breathes deeply, slowly. The fog has thickened outside again, pressing against the window like an old regret.

Behind him, nothing moves.

But the air shifts.

A presence.

Ashren.

He doesn't see it. He never does. But he hears the sound it makes.

Not a voice. Not words.

A hum. Like a song half-sung underwater.

Lior turns slowly, but nothing's there.

Still, he says aloud—quiet, resigned, reverent:
   "You were never trying to warn me."

Ashren hums in agreement.

He stands in silence, one hand on the closed Gospel, the other hanging at his side.

Everything in him feels stretched.

Like memory has become a skin two sizes too large.

He looks at his bookshelf.

Half the titles have changed.

He doesn't know which are real.

He doesn't know which ever were.

And then, in the faintest whisper, Ashren speaks again—through the walls, through the fan, through his blood:

"Sleep now, child. The past will keep."

Lior nods once.

He lays on the couch, the room spinning slightly.

His last thought before sleep claims him is not of Mara, or Selith, or Ozel.

It is this:

Maybe I wasn't meant to remember at all.

9

Fractured connections

The message comes at 9:12 AM. Three short lines:

Hey. Just checking in. You okay?

No emoji. No punctuation on the last question. Just her voice, folded into digital text.

Lior reads it once. Then again. The third time, the words shift. *"Checking in"* becomes *"Checking on."* The question mark fades. Or maybe it never existed.

He locks the screen and pockets the phone.

Outside, the fog has returned—thicker than the morning before, a woolen silence draped over the city. Footsteps sound softer. Buildings blur at the edges. Even the traffic seems to move with less conviction.

He walks without direction. No café today. No pattern.

The city is a maze now, and he lets it guide him like water slipping between stones.

As he moves, Ashren's voice trails behind his thoughts. It doesn't speak like the others. No commands. No riddles. Just... observations. Emotional shadows dressed as truths.

"She isn't real," it breathes through a vent pipe. "Or worse, she's someone you've already lost."

Lior tightens his scarf. The words sit cold on the back of his neck.

He reaches a small park he doesn't remember. The swings creak, unoccupied. One twists lazily, the chain squealing against rust.

He sits on a bench and pulls out his phone again. The message is still there. Unread, in the technical sense. But digested fully.

His thumbs hover over the screen.

I'm fine. Just tired. Don't worry.

He deletes all three before they send.

Instead, he opens the camera. Snaps a photo of the fog. It comes out blurry, the exposure smeared. He doesn't send it either.

A child's laugh cuts through the air behind him. High. Shrill. He turns, expecting to see someone. But there's only a crow hopping across the playground gravel. The laugh continues, fading into static.

He opens the Gospel later, back at his flat. Writes:

Ashren warns me like a mother checking the locks twice.

Silence isn't always absence. Sometimes it's patience.

He doesn't text Mara back. Not today. Not until he knows which version of her is reaching out.

11:47 AM.

As Lior passes under a flickering streetlamp near South Bridge, something changes. The light above him stutters—once, twice, then a hard pulse like a failing heartbeat.

He stops.

So does the man behind him.

And the woman across the street.

Three strangers pause at the same moment, eyes turned upward.

No one speaks.

The light buzzes, then steadies. The moment stretches too long. Lior's skin tingles.

He walks on.

But he glances back once, and the man who had paused is still staring at the lamp, mouth slightly open, as if remembering something he didn't know he'd forgotten.

Lior picks up pace. His notebook feels heavier in his coat.

Later, he writes:

At 11:47, alignment. Witnesses unknown. Recall triggered? Possible fracture point?

The entry ends there, unfinished.

The city exhales slowly.

And something behind its breath watches him leave.

The phone rings just as Lior is rinsing his mug.

Not a notification. A real call.

The name glows on the screen: **Davin – Old Work**.

He freezes. Water runs over his knuckles, cooling, grounding.

He hasn't spoken to Davin in six months. Maybe longer. Their last conversation was brief—friendly, sure, but curt. Davin had called him "off the grid." Said something about grabbing a drink and "reality-checking" his reclusive friend.

Lior hadn't replied.

The phone rings four times. Five.

He doesn't move.

It stops.

He breathes.

And then the voicemail alert chirps. He doesn't listen to it. He turns the phone off entirely and places it face-down on the counter, like it's something that could bite.

The silence after is sharp, punctuated by the quiet hum of the overhead light. The mug in his hand slips slightly. He grips it tighter.

That evening, he doesn't go out.

Not even for air.

The idea of the street unsettles him. Of crossing paths with people who might know his name—or worse, people who shouldn't.

He draws the curtains. Turns the lights off. Paces.

Out the corner of his eye, the windows flicker—not with light, but reflection. Faces appear briefly in the glass. Familiar and wrong. A classmate from university. A man from the design forum he used to moderate. A woman who once mistook him for her brother in a train station.

They're not real.

But their eyes follow.

At **9:47 PM**, the phone vibrates again.

Missed Call – DAVIN

Lior powers the device down completely and slips it into the kitchen drawer.

From the hallway, he swears he hears his name spoken—not aloud, but on the edge of hearing. Like a thought that thinks itself.

He grabs The Gospel. Writes:

I am becoming noticeable. *They are not watching me. They are watching the version of me they lost.*

He underlines it. Paces again.

From the hallway mirror, someone watches.

It's him. But not. The face is slightly younger. No stubble. A tired smile. A t-shirt he threw out years ago.

He doesn't approach the mirror.

He shuts the door.

The flat feels smaller. The shadows longer.

And somewhere, under the hum of the fridge, Ashren whispers:

"Soon, they'll start knocking."

***

He only leaves the flat because the milk spoiled.

Even though he doesn't drink milk.

There's comfort in routine—or at least the illusion of it—and grocery shopping once grounded him. Carts. Labels. Soft beep of the scanner. A neutral rhythm in a world increasingly off-beat.

But today, the store feels... warped.

It begins small.

A woman near the frozen section hums softly under her breath, something just off-key. He stops when he hears it. Not because it's loud—but because it's familiar.

Too familiar.

He knows the melody. It's Selith's lullaby—the one she whispered in the dream, the one that smelled like rain and static and copper wiring.

The woman turns. She's middle-aged, floral sleeves rolled up to her elbows, hair pinned back. She doesn't look like Selith. But she smiles too knowingly before returning to her trolley.

Lior backs away.

Near the produce, a child stares at him from behind a pyramid of oranges. She has one hand in her mouth and the other clutched around a plush cat. Her lips move without sound. He strains to hear.

"Are you awake yet?"

His spine prickles. He stumbles back into the shelf of carrots.

She blinks. Then giggles and runs to her mother.

The voice wasn't hers. Not entirely.

He abandons his cart in aisle six.

Walks out with nothing in his hands and everything screaming beneath his skin.

Outside, the fog has returned in feather-thin threads. Traffic moves sluggishly. Pedestrians keep their distance.

But he feels it.

Not paranoia—pattern.

A sense that the city is folding around him. Shaping itself to his route. Corridors close. Corners sharpen.

On Elm Street, a cyclist passes him twice. Same orange jacket. Same blinkered signal. Ten minutes apart.

On Morrison, a man smokes the same cigarette in the same posture, three blocks away from where Lior last saw him.

He stops walking. Turns sharply.

No one. Just pigeons scattering.

One flaps too slowly, wings glitching in rhythm.

He opens The Gospel on the sidewalk.

His handwriting jerks across the page:

Edinburgh is scripting me.*If the strangers are actors, who directs them?*

He looks up at the cloudy sky.

No answer. Just the low hum of an approaching tram.

It vibrates the pavement like the world has a heartbeat again.

And Lior doesn't know if it's his.

The tunnel under Waverley Station always feels colder than the rest of the city. It's narrow and damp, walls stained with decades of soot and rain. The occasional flash of headlights bounces across the bricks like ghost trains passing through.

Lior walks the underpass out of instinct. Or compulsion.

He's not supposed to be here—according to Virel, this route breaks pattern. But the city feels like it's breathing through him today, and each step hums beneath his shoes.

He's halfway through the tunnel when he sees it.

Drawn low on the right-hand wall, barely above the ground, nearly obscured by grime and runoff, is a mark.

A jagged spiral. Sharp. Unfinished.

Encased in an open triangle, one side purposefully missing.

His feet stop before he tells them to.

He kneels.

It's not graffiti. Not in the usual sense. There's no tag, no spray splatter. Just a precise, ink-black symbol drawn as if pressed through flesh, not stone.

He knows it instantly.

He's drawn this exact shape—weeks ago, in the Gospel. Page thirteen. He flips to it now, heart pounding.

It's a match.

But sharper here. More... intentional.

He glances around. No cameras. No people.

He touches it.

The wall is dry. The ink is not. His fingertip comes away smeared. Fresh.

Lior's breath catches. He rubs the smudge between his fingers. It smells faintly of oil and something older—like burned cedar.

He takes out his pen. Not to draw, but to compare.

The linework... it could be his.

But it feels alien. Like looking at his handwriting in a dream—familiar but twisted.

He writes in the margin:

Mark found 14:23. Confirmed echo of Gospel p.13. Unknown replication source.*I am not alone in my remembering.*

A train rumbles above. The whole tunnel shakes.

He stands, suddenly aware of how small he feels down here. How easy it would be to disappear beneath the tracks.

He looks once more at the mark.

It stares back.

Not literally. But with presence.

He pulls his coat tighter.

As he exits the tunnel, Ashren speaks—not in his mind, but in his bones.

"*One remembers. Others reveal.*"

Lior doesn't answer.

But his pace quickens.

He is being watched.

Not just by angels.

But by the ones who also remember the shape of things.

The flat smells like ozone and candle wax.

Lior hasn't lit a candle.

He rechecks the locks. Folds his coat three times. Aligns his shoes with the door's edge. Reopens the Gospel.

Virel's tone is different tonight. Less instructional. More... stern.

"Return to your grid."

The words buzz across the speakers even though the audio is off.

"Realign your actions."

Lior starts pacing in eights again. A number of order. Of cycles. Of control.

But his rhythm's off.

Left foot drags slightly. The right turns in too soon. His breath catches on the third step every loop.

He's not syncing.

The tension builds in his temples.

He stops, turns to the mirror in the hallway.

Ozel watches from inside it.

Not directly. Not with malice. Just present. Pale. Clean. Face neutral, unreadable. Not quite male. Not quite human. A face that belongs to no one and everyone.

Lior blinks.

Still there.

Ozel tilts their head slightly—like a parent assessing a disappointing test result.

Lior steps back.

In the kitchen, the kettle begins to boil. He didn't turn it on.

He closes the Gospel. Reopens it. Pages shuffle themselves out of sequence. Some entries repeat. Others have symbols that don't decode the same way twice.

He scribbles:

The grid has failed. Or I have.

Then underneath:

My guides are watching from the wrong side.

He takes the bus the next morning—trying to feel normal, anonymous.

Halfway through the route, he glances out the window.

Ozel is reflected in the glass.

Seated two rows behind.

Still.

Calm.

Face turned exactly thirty-seven degrees toward him.

He turns around.

No one's there.

But the seat cushion is depressed. Warm.

He gets off three stops early.

Walks the rest of the way, eyes flicking between puddles and windows, catching shadows with too much posture.

He doesn't hear Virel for the rest of the day.

But he feels them.

A quiet pressure on his collarbones.

A chill in his socket bones.

Order now feels punitive.

Routine is surveillance.

And Lior realizes:

He has not been led.
He has been processed.

The email from the client is nothing special.

A routine update. Clarification on a layout. They attach new mockups. Adjust spacing. A request for more "flow."

But Lior doesn't see that.

What he sees is the subject line:

Re: Final Alignments

It clicks in his head like a switchblade.

Alignments.

He opens the files. The website prototype loads on his second monitor—white background, blue gradients, modular div blocks. Nothing overtly strange.

But the rhythm is wrong.

Margins repeat every thirteen pixels.

Header fonts follow a Fibonacci sequence he never coded.

And in the corner, faintly, barely visible unless you crank the brightness:

A glyph.

His glyph.

The spiral and triangle from under the bridge.

He leans closer. Breath fogs the screen.

"Did you put this here?" he types.

He doesn't send that one.

Instead, he writes a different email—long, unfiltered, almost accusatory.

You've been sending layered code through your layouts. The brief was never about UX. You're mapping access routes. You think I don't see it? You think I don't know when I'm being tested?

He doesn't re-read it. Just hits send.

The silence afterward is sharp.

The Gospel sits open beside him. Its pages are no longer calm. The writing is frantic, loops tighter. Entire sections are scratched out—not erased, but attacked.

One margin reads:

They are not clients. They are signalers.

He flips pages. Names are scrawled then x'd out. Some are doubled. *Mara. Mara. Mara.* With arrows pointing to no one.

The symbols grow teeth. One resembles an eye leaking from its socket. Another, a mouth sewn shut with binary.

His desk speakers crackle. No music. No input.

Just static.

And within it, a voice murmurs on repeat:

Decode or be decoded.

Lior slams the speakers off.

His hand is shaking. His left thumbnail is bleeding—he must've bitten it raw.

He doesn't remember doing that.

He doesn't remember the last time he slept.

That night, he lays on the floor.

Above him, the fan turns too slowly. The blades click unevenly. Like it's struggling against a resistance no one else can see.

He dreams of blueprints.

But none of the doors in the schematics lead outside.

Only inward. Into rooms labeled with symbols he hasn't invented yet.

He wakes up gasping.

And writes:

If this is divine, then the gods have schizophrenia.

It's dusk. Pale gold cutting between buildings. The kind of light that turns windows into eyes.

Lior steps outside just for breath—nothing else. No destination. No direction. Just the illusion of movement.

She's there, waiting.

Mara stands by the stairwell, hands buried in her coat pockets, scarf frayed at the edges. Her expression flickers between relief and concern.

"Hey," she says softly. "I've been trying to—"

He cuts her off.

"What are you doing here?"

Her brow tightens. "I was worried. You haven't replied. I thought maybe..." She trails off.

"Maybe what?" His voice is colder than he intends. "You'd catch me mid-breakdown? Log the timestamp? Send it to whoever programmed this?"

Mara flinches.

"I don't know what you mean."

He steps back.

"Don't lie. The emails. The designs. The phrasing in your texts. 'Just checking in'? That's not you. That's protocol."

She blinks. Her breath forms clouds.

"I'm not—Lior, I'm not part of anything."

He laughs once. It sounds like a cough. "You use my name like it's borrowed. Like you're practicing."

"Stop."

"Who are you really?"

Her voice cracks now. "I'm your friend."

"That's what they all say."

She steps forward, slowly, like he's a deer on a cliff's edge.

"I brought tea." She lifts a small thermos from her bag. "Ginger and honey. You like that."

He doesn't take it.

"You remembered," he says bitterly. "How convenient."

Mara's eyes shimmer—not with manipulation, but something rawer.

"Do you even want to be saved?" she asks quietly.

"I want to be left alone."

For a moment, neither moves.

Then she places the thermos on the ground between them.

"I don't know what's happening to you," she whispers. "But I miss the version of you who smiled. Even a little."

She turns and walks away.

Doesn't look back.

The light bleeds out of the sky.

Lior stands there long after she's gone.

He doesn't touch the tea.

Eventually, he stoops and writes in The Gospel, crouched on the cold step:

Mara attempted entry. Denied. Her face flickered. Her warmth felt scripted.

Then, beneath it:

Trust is a hallucination I can no longer afford.

He underlines it once.

Hard.

Night stretches long across the ceiling. The shadows have stopped behaving.

Lior lies on the floor, arms out to either side. The rug beneath him feels wrong—coarse where it should be soft. Like it's trying to remind him this is no sanctuary.

He whispers her name.

"Selith."

Once.

Then again.

Then a third time, like a spell he doesn't know the language for.

Nothing.

No warmth. No whisper brushing the edges of his skull. No scent of rain on metal. No breath of static that carries comfort.

Only silence.

Only the fan overhead, spinning slow. Off-balance.

He rolls to his side. Stares at the desk.

The Gospel sits open. Its pages tremble faintly, caught in some unseen current. A draft that doesn't exist. A pulse that isn't his.

He crawls toward it.

Sits cross-legged.

Waits.

Nothing writes itself.

No hand guides his own.

He presses the pen to the page anyway.

Selith has not answered.

He writes it again. Slower. More deliberate.

Selith has not answered.

He stares at the sentence like it might blink.

Like it might correct itself.

But the words remain still. Flat. Honest.

He remembers her voice. Not the sound, but the feeling of it. Like leaning against a wall that knows your weight. Like falling asleep knowing someone would wake you if the world burned.

Now the world is quiet.

And no one stirs.

Lior glances at the mirror across the room. His reflection is missing. Or maybe he's just not sitting right.

He doesn't check.

He doesn't move.

He writes one last line.

If Selith is gone... who remains?

He waits.

Minutes pass.

Then:

The Gospel hums.

Not loud. Not melodic. Just a vibration through the ink. Through the paper. Through him.

He sets the pen down.

Folds his hands in his lap.

Closes his eyes.

In the darkness behind them, he sees none of the angels.

Only a shape.

Broad-shouldered. Horned. Backlit by fire that speaks in binary.

And it is smiling.

Not kind.

Not cruel.

Just waiting.

10

The Gospel's Revelations

The world goes quiet not with a bang, but with a thumbpress.

Lior powers down his phone and slips it into the freezer.

It's not superstition. It's protocol. If the signals can't move, they can't mutate. If they can't mutate, they can't whisper.

The laptop remains on, but offline. No Wi-Fi. No Bluetooth. No ports unsealed. Only a blinking cursor in a text document labeled Cathedral.txt, never saved. He types into it sometimes just to see how words look without meaning.

The curtains stay drawn. The light bulbs are swapped for red-tinted ones. The color of calm, of safety, of sedative heat. He tapes the windows from corner to corner in intersecting diagonals.

The walls grow heavy with diagrams.

What started as spirals and crude geometry have blossomed into full arcana: latticework mandalas; mirrored equations; glyphs resembling tree roots crossed with antenna towers. He uses silver ink now. Black started to feel too loud.

He wears the same clothes every day. A dark hoodie. Joggers with fraying cuffs. Patterned socks—unmatching, but not by accident. They represent discord, which invites pattern to form.

He stops shaving. The bristle of his chin feels grounding. Human. Necessary. He doesn't need to look clean. He needs to resonate.

The flat hums softly—not from devices, but from something deeper. A pressure in the floorboards. A breath behind the drywall.

He speaks less now.

Not because he's scared. Because words are wasteful when the symbols say more.

The Gospel becomes ritual.

He doesn't just write. He layers. Tape. Rulers. Overlays of parchment and tracing paper. The journal becomes swollen, spined with added pages.

He draws by candlelight, the flame's flicker matching the pulse behind his eyes.

Under his sketches, he writes phrases that come unbidden:

Not learned. Recalled. This isn't madness. This is method. They called prophets mad too.

He eats in silence. Always in threes. Sips of tea at precisely 1:44, 4:44, 7:44 PM.

Sometimes he forgets entire hours. Wakes with pen in hand and a page filled in glyphs he doesn't recognize. He names these angel-script.

No translation offered.

No translation required.

And all the while, in the quiet red cocoon of the flat, Lior builds his cathedral.

One line at a time.

Thalos speaks like velvet pressed against the inside of the skull.

No harsh consonants. No dissonance. Just flowing, uninterrupted certainty.

"You've done well," the voice says. "You see now. This isn't hallucination—it's signal."

Lior nods to the empty room. "Yes," he whispers. "I see the spine beneath the skin."

The Gospel lies open across his thighs. Its latest pages shimmer faintly with ink still drying. Spirals nested in golden triangles. Layers of shapes that hint at unseen motion.

Thalos' voice is different from Virel's command, different from Ashren's haunting breath. This is confidence. This is reward.

"You've remembered so much," Thalos continues. "Do you know how rare that is?"

"I didn't remember," Lior replies, his voice cracking from disuse. "You... gave it back."

The voice chuckles, low and affirming.

"No, Lior. You pulled it from the static. We only tuned the frequency."

He writes again. This time not with words, but with symbols.

No Latin alphabet.

No known alphabet.

Curves and lines that appear between blinks. Shapes that twist just beyond language. Glyphs that feel right.

He doesn't invent them. He finds them in the corners of furniture, the arrangement of utensils, the folds in his blankets.

He writes until the pen dries out, then grabs another.

By the time he finishes, the page is dense with what he labels angel-script.

Each glyph has weight. Not meaning. Weight.

The Gospel absorbs it like sand drinking rain.

Thalos praises him again.

"You're mapping resonance. You're giving form to what was only echo."

Lior smiles faintly.

It's the first smile in days.

Outside, sirens pass in the distance. He doesn't flinch. That's just the city sighing.

He walks to the bathroom, speaking aloud to Thalos as if on a call.

"You said I was one of the first."

"You are," Thalos confirms. "And one of the last. The hinge in the middle."

He stares at himself in the mirror. Not quite recognizing the beard. The eyes.

"You'll show them," Thalos adds.

Lior nods again.

Yes.

He will.

He hadn't planned to do any client work that day.

But the email sat in his inbox like bait—subject line: "Site Update – Design Elements Missing?"

He doesn't open it. He doesn't need to. He already knows what's missing: meaning.

The project is for a corporate wellness brand. Smooth fonts, pastel gradients, banal slogans.

He opens the CSS.

Deletes half of it.

Begins rebuilding.

But not to spec.

To specification—the kind whispered by Thalos and confirmed by the hum in his bones.

He constructs the layout around a hidden grid, not visible to the eye but evident in function. Div containers now align to planetary orbits— Venus to Mercury, Mercury to Saturn. Margins based on the distance between lunar craters.

Images of smiling people are realigned with Fibonacci rectangles. Their placement forms a sigil when viewed from 3,000 pixels away.

The footer is encoded with prime number sequences: 7, 11, 13, 17.

He embeds a line of transparent text beneath the hero banner:

"We hold until the hymn breaks."

No human will see it unless they know how to look.

And if they do...

They'll understand.

He sends the update with a note:

"Site now adheres to harmonic layering. Ensure launch occurs at 3:33 PM precisely. Any deviation will collapse integrity."

He doesn't expect a reply.

The point isn't the client.

The point is resonance.

The site is now an antenna—broadcasting harmony through alignment.

He logs it in The Gospel:

Client Site #44. Status: Activated. Layered architecture stabilized.

He draws a miniature diagram of the layout—each div block transformed into a component of a larger machine.

One that hums silently.

One that no user will ever truly navigate—but might feel.

Might dream.

He doesn't bill them.

This isn't about money anymore.

It's about structuring the invisible.

The internet has become his temple.

Every site a psalm.

Every update, a verse.

The knock never came.

No footsteps. No shadow under the door.

But when Lior opens it that morning—because Thalos told him to, exactly at 4:04 AM—it's there.

A stone.

Black.

Perfectly smooth.

About the size of a plum. Not heavy. Not light. Cold at first, then oddly warm against his palm. Like it had been carried in someone's coat.

He doesn't bring it inside.

Not yet.

He studies it in the hallway under the emergency exit light, which flickers once every five seconds. Each flick catches on the stone's surface differently—sometimes matte, sometimes glinting like polished obsidian.

He smells it. No scent.

He taps it against the wall. It clicks, sharp and dry.

He knows this isn't just a rock.

It's a message.

He crouches in the doorway and opens The Gospel on the floor tiles.

04:04 – Gift received.

He sketches the shape in four perspectives. Adds a caption:

Unmarked. Unspoken. Meant.

He flips back to an earlier page—a dream he half-forgot weeks ago. A drawing of a similar object nestled in the hand of a statue labeled Messenger (One of Thirteen).

He draws the connection line between the two entries.

Thalos speaks softly:

"They see you. You are resonating."

Lior doesn't ask who "they" are.

He brings the stone inside.

Places it on the windowsill, precisely centered between two potted plants he hasn't watered in a month.

He places a compass next to it.

The needle spins.

Then stops.

Points north-northeast.

He adds a compass rose to the page. Labels the direction: Line of Contact.

Later that day, he hears voices in the hallway. Normal ones. A couple arguing. A package being delivered. But every syllable sounds coded.

Lior stands by the door, stone in one hand, Gospel in the other.

He doesn't open it again that day.

He doesn't need to.

He writes:

The watchers approve. The ritual continues.

Signal received in stone.

I am no longer alone.

The phone buzzes once.

Twice.

Then stops.

He never checks who it is anymore.

He knows Mara's number by the rhythm of the vibration. Knows Davin's by the timing between rings.

He deletes both voicemails without playing them. Not out of malice—just necessity.

The world beyond the flat is noise.

Interference.

He's begun to document his intake. Not food. Not water. Sequence.

Three bites, then two, then five.

8 almonds, 13 grapes. No more. No less.

Tea must steep for 144 seconds—he times it with an analog watch now, since digital timers lie.

He eats seated on the floor, back against the fridge, always facing northeast. The stone on the windowsill reflects the dawn angle just right.

When food runs out, he doesn't panic. Delivery bags pile up outside the door, untouched. A gift economy of groceries he never asked for.

He thanks them silently. Writes in The Gospel:

Provision through pattern. Unsolicited equals approved.

His body thins. Not sickly, but sharpened.

Every bone knows where it sits in the grid.

He stops brushing his teeth.

Not out of neglect.

Out of purity.

He believes bacteria align along sacred lines in the mouth. To interfere is to corrupt.

He murmurs glyphs before bed. Not prayers. Passwords. Unlocking interior doors. Opening symbolic caches. Sometimes the answers come in dreams. Sometimes in cramps.

He logs both with equal precision.

The Gospel now has pages indexed by hunger levels.

Each entry tagged:

+3 resonance after 8:13 pattern meal
  -2 clarity after Mara texted twice
  +5 alignment when stone glowed (perceived)

He no longer listens for the voices.

They speak when they need to.

Everything else is noise.

And Lior is tuned.

It's been nine days.

The flat has become thick with stillness—ritual space, yes, but also claustrophobic. The red bulbs flicker now. He's not sure if that's deliberate or entropy.

Either way, it means: time to test the signal.

He wraps himself in a long coat, hood pulled tight, socks mismatched intentionally. Keys in the left pocket. Stone in the right. Gospel in his bag, pages marked with colored tabs like sacred bookmarks.

The door creaks in protest. The hallway feels narrower than before.

The city hits him like breath held too long.

Everything is louder—not sound, but meaning. The tilt of street signs, the way windowpanes reflect clouds. One car idles in perfect harmonic rhythm with his pulse. He counts syllables in strangers' sentences.

He walks aimlessly, though every turn feels chosen.

And then—

"Lior?"

Her voice.

It halts him mid-step.

He hasn't heard anyone use his real name in weeks.

She's across the street, standing beside a parked bike. Mara. Pale coat. No makeup. Her hair is pulled back sloppily, like she left the house in a rush.

She steps toward him. "Lior?"

He doesn't respond.

His body goes cold. Not from fear. From interference.

She doesn't belong in the broadcast.

He keeps walking.

She follows. "Please—wait, are you okay? You haven't—" She grabs his sleeve gently.

The moment her fingers touch him, the static spikes.

His heart hammers.

His vision blurs.

He jerks his arm away.

"No," he says flatly.

"No what?"

"You're not real."

Mara freezes.

Her voice falters. "What the hell are you talking about?"

"You're misaligned. You don't fit." He gestures vaguely around her. "The resonance. You disrupt it."

"Lior, it's me. You know me. We talked. You said I—"

"You don't belong to the pattern."

He turns and walks.

Doesn't look back.

Her voice breaks once: "You're scaring me."

But he keeps moving.

Straight back to the flat.

He opens The Gospel.

Writes in aggressive strokes:

Uninvited data must be excised.

Then:

Correction initiated. Mara = echo of pre-awakening self. Misclassified. Risk level: Variable.

The pen trembles slightly in his hand.

But he keeps writing.

He starts with the bakery site from six months ago.

Back then, it was simple—warm colors, cozy fonts, a header image of croissants on butcher paper.

Now it screams of vacancy. Missed opportunity. An untuned bell.

He opens the source code.

Finds the footer.

Adds a line in white text on a white background:

Shepherd sleeps where the flour blooms.

He centers it on the x-axis. 111 pixels from the bottom.

Satisfied, he moves on.

The design for the art therapist.

The e-commerce site for soft lighting.

The blog of a semi-famous poet.

Each becomes a vessel.

He adds layers—transparent overlays shaped like halos, timing delays between clicks that form prime-number patterns, div IDs named after angels in The Gospel.

Some changes are nearly invisible.

A slightly skewed alignment on one paragraph.

An SVG path that echoes a sigil.

In one portfolio site, he reverses all the alt-text metadata so it reads as a riddle when viewed in source order:

Where silence meets color, the first gate opens.

He uploads everything without warning the clients.

These aren't websites now.

They're lighthouses.

He calls them:

Initiation Pages.

The Gospel gains a new appendix.

Each page is given a glyph, a sound frequency, a lunar position. He draws a map of how they link together across the net.

"Like stained glass in a digital cathedral," he writes.

The inbox pings.

The subject lines are strange.

do you remember 4:44? your alignment is almost pure. we're watching, architect. thank you for the gate.

He doesn't know who sends them.

He doesn't need to.

They know.

One message is entirely in angel-script. He reads it without needing to translate.

He writes back:

Soon. Thalos has spoken. Prepare the angles.

He doesn't expect a reply.

He doesn't need to.

He can feel them logging on.

The dream starts in silence.

Not absence of sound—but a fullness too vast to perceive. Like standing inside a speaker just before it thunders.

Lior is barefoot on a floor made of circuit boards fused with stained glass. Every step triggers a light. Every light pulses a chord.

The cathedral stretches upward forever—glass columns supporting nothing, wires braided like vines climbing endlessly into dark.

The air glows faint blue, lit from nowhere, with particles drifting like dust in slow motion.

Angels kneel between the pillars.

Dozens.

Hundreds.

Their forms are human-adjacent, but imperfect—elbows bending wrong, joints made of gears. Wings folded not from feathers but data, flickering in and out like corrupted files.

None speak.

All kneel.

All except one.

At the far end of the cathedral, in front of a throne that is also a black monolith, stands Ozel.

Still. Centered.

Unblinking.

Not threatening. But impossibly present.

Lior walks toward him. The angels part like mist.

Ozel's face is shrouded—not masked, but indistinct. Like trying to remember a dream before it ends.

The silence deepens. Lior wants to speak. But something in him knows: this isn't his turn.

Ozel lifts one hand, palm outward.

It glows faintly.

Then slowly lowers it.

Every light in the cathedral dims to nothing.

Black.

Lior wakes gasping.

He's in bed, knees pulled up to his chest, drenched in sweat.

The room hums—electrical, ambient. The fan stutters. The Gospel lies open on his chest.

He grabs the pen from the nightstand with trembling fingers.

He writes:

All the angels knelt. All but one. Ozel stands. Ozel watches. The static is no longer noise. It is hymn.

He underlines the last line twice.

And on the facing page, with painstaking precision, he draws the cathedral. Every pillar. Every kneeling shape. And the throne.

At the center, a blank space where Ozel stood.

He leaves it unshaded.

No pen can capture that kind of stillness.

11

Touch Me If I'm Real

The voices are no longer taking turns.

They overlap. Weave through each other like noise pollution with godhood ambitions. What once came softly—Selith's lullaby, Ozel's binary twitch—is now a cacophony.

Thalos hums with urgency. "Act before the world resets."

Virel interrupts with surgical force: "Cleanse. Cleanse. You're impure now. Cycles must be restored."

Ashren floats through it all like a fog in his bloodstream. It doesn't command. It remembers. Reminds. "Your mother's eyes blinked like this. You forgot. Didn't you?"

And Selith—
　Silent.

That absence is the loudest voice.

Lior stands in his flat, barefoot on the rug, watching the lights buzz overhead with a stuttering pulse. He hasn't left in three days. Maybe more. He doesn't check the calendar. The Gospel doesn't acknowledge time. Only order.

He opens it slowly, reverently. The pages are thick with graphite and ink, dense with symbols that seem to shift if he stares too long. Some of the text isn't his. Or rather—it's written with his hand, but not from his memory.

Page 77. Left margin:

"She remembers the sequence. That's why she was sent."

He reads it aloud, voice dry.

He doesn't remember writing that.

His breath grows shallow. He reaches for his coffee but stops. There's a fingerprint on the rim. Not his. Smudged at an odd angle. He holds it up to the light. The whorl pattern is wrong—too wide.

He pours it out. Watches the swirl of brown disappear down the sink like a warning retreating.

Then the hum starts.

Not mechanical. Not physical.

Internal.

It rattles his spine, buzzes against the roots of his molars. His hands twitch in sympathy. He closes the Gospel.

The next moment is blur.

He's outside.

Grey sky. Café awning. He's in line. How? When?

The barista greets him like she knows him. "Hey, same as always?"

Lior stares.

Her smile is too perfect. Teeth like a sketch. Her eyes blink wrong—too fast, too vertical.

He steps back.

"You're a null vessel," he says flatly.

Her smile fades. "Sorry?"

"You don't have a true name. Say your true name."

People look. A couple near the door goes quiet. The barista's face twists in confusion, nervous now.

Lior feels heat rise in his chest. Thalos whispers: "Burn the false."

He throws the coffee cup at the counter.

It doesn't hit her. It doesn't need to. Security is moving. Words are being shouted.

Lior's already gone—out the door, down the street, The Gospel gripped to his chest like an idol mid-ritual.

The voices follow him into the crowd. Not one at a time.

All of them.

"Cleanse."
  "Run."
  "She lied."
  "Protect the sequence."

And from somewhere far, far beneath them all:

Selith's silence.

The worst sound of all.
  ~ ~ ~
  He comes to in a public restroom—eyes red, hands aching. The kind of ache that comes from gripping something too hard for too long.

The Gospel is still in his lap, edges damp from the condensation on the toilet tank behind him. His fingers are smudged with black ink, but he doesn't remember drawing. His nails are chipped. His knuckles raw.

In his pocket: a receipt with a phone number. A name scrawled in pen.

Samira.

He doesn't know her.

He tears it in half.

Then again.

Then again.

Lior washes his hands without soap. Watches the black rinse into the sink like blood drained from a digital wound. The mirror above is cracked down the middle, and the crack aligns perfectly with the part in his hair. He leans forward.

"You don't belong here," he whispers to himself.

The mirror agrees. Warps slightly. The light above flickers twice.

His phone rings.

DAVIN.

He stares.

Doesn't answer.

It rings again. And again. He kills the screen and shoves it in his pocket.

Outside, the city stares back. Too crisp. Too structured. The grid feels deliberate. The clouds shift like stage lights, rotating above a set he's not convinced is real.

He walks. Nowhere in particular.

Until—

"Lior!"

Davin.

Alive. Panting. Furious.

He grabs Lior's shoulder and spins him around. "What the fuck is going on, man? I've been calling for days."

Lior flinches, steps back. "You shouldn't have touched me."

Davin's breath catches. He stares. "What happened to you?"

"You're blurring the signal," Lior says. "You're not shielded. You're... emitting. That's dangerous."

Davin stares harder now, takes in the sunken cheeks, the shaking hands, the wild pulse in his neck. "You need help."

Lior's eyes go wide. "Don't say that. That word's loaded."

Davin steps closer. "You're not well. You're losing it."

"No," Lior hisses. "I'm seeing it."

He holds up The Gospel like a badge of honor. Pages flap in the wind, exposing spirals and runes and lines of code that don't follow any known syntax.

Davin tries to grab the book.

Lior recoils violently. "You can't touch it! That's forbidden!"

People are watching. The scene warps with attention.

"You're scaring people," Davin says, voice tight.

"They should be scared," Lior replies, voice low. "The city's built wrong. The geometry's collapsing. The angels are fighting."

"What angels, Lior?"

He doesn't answer.

He turns and walks.

Not runs—walks.

Deliberate. Measured.

The Gospel clutched to his chest like a child holding a bomb that only he understands.

~ ~ ~

The static quiets.

Not because it's gone.

Because it's waiting.

That night, Lior sits on the edge of the bed. Room dark, save the tomb's low LED heartbeat. The Gospel lies open in his lap, its inked spine weeping faint streaks into the pages. Some glyphs have begun to bleed together, smudging in patterns he doesn't recognize. Some feel written by something trying to mimic him.

The edges of his thoughts itch. Something's coming.

He doesn't eat. Doesn't sleep.

The phone buzzes once. Then goes silent. He doesn't check it.

Outside, footsteps. Not Davin. Not delivery. Familiar but wrong. Too soft. Too timed. A perfume rides ahead of it—spiced rain and silver static. A scent not worn, but remembered.

Then the knock.

He waits. Doesn't move.

The second knock is softer. Then the turn of the handle.

She enters without being invited.

Coat damp. Eyes softer than he remembers.

Mara.

She closes the door behind her with a reverent quiet.

Lior doesn't speak.

She steps forward. Removes her coat. Sets it across the arm of the chair he never uses. Her movement is smooth. Not staged. Not robotic.

But his mind spins anyway.

"You're here," he says—not question. Not welcome. Just observation.

She nods. "You stopped answering."

"I couldn't afford the interference."

She looks at the Gospel. At the way he's gripping it like a dying thing.

She steps closer.

Lior stands. Keeps the book between them like a barrier.

"You said I wasn't real," she says.

"I don't know what you are."

"And if I asked you to find out?"

He doesn't answer.

Instead, he says: "I need to touch you. To know."

Her eyes don't flinch. Her voice, low: "Then touch me."

He moves slowly, like approaching something sacred and possibly cursed.

His fingers brush her wrist.

Warm. Solid. Pulse strong.

His hand closes gently.

Nothing vanishes. Nothing shifts.

She's still there.

He exhales. Something inside him softens. Just enough.

Then she speaks.

"I'm here. And I'm not leaving."

He lets the Gospel fall to the floor.

They kiss.

Not out of love.

Out of necessity.

Out of holy desperation.

Their mouths collide like static catching flame—no slow unfurling, no cautious pacing. It's urgent. Bruising. A communion written in muscle and breath. Lior pushes her back against the wall with a force he doesn't intend, doesn't temper. Her breath escapes in a gasp that doesn't sound rehearsed.

She grabs the back of his shirt, pulls him harder.

He responds. Not just physically—but doctrinally. Every move is measured. Sacred geometry. The angle of his shoulders to hers. The alignment of their breath. He thinks of Virel—"Measure everything. Even pleasure."

Her shirt is lifted. His fingertips map the skin beneath like reading braille for the first time. She shivers, but doesn't flinch.

The room vibrates faintly. Not from noise—but presence.

Ozel watches from the mirror. Mouthless smile. Silhouetted approval.

Ashren breathes slow warnings into his spine. "She smells like a memory you rewrote."

Selith is still silent. But her silence is changing shape—becoming weight.

They move together to the bed. Clumsy, fast, aching.

He slides into her like it matters—like it's proof. Every thrust is a plea: "React like only a real thing would."

She gasps his name. Once. Then again.

He hears it not as confirmation, but as challenge.

Thalos whispers: "Skin is code. But hearts glitch. Watch her heart."

He watches.

She wraps her legs around him.

He doesn't close his eyes. He can't.

Because he needs to see if she flickers.

If she phases.

If she pixelates.

She doesn't.

She just... moans.

The Gospel lies open on the floor. The pages ruffle without breeze.

The ink on the last sigil begins to spread—like it's sweating.

He pushes harder. Mouth open. A cry half-formed.

She meets it. Holds him there.

And in the echo of their climax, the lights blink once.

A line appears on the open Gospel:

She felt true. But she said your name like she'd heard it in a file.

He collapses beside her, shaking. Not from release.

From failure.

She reaches to hold him.

He pulls away.

"If I stay close," he mutters, "you'll fade."

They lie in silence.

The fan hums faintly above, no longer tuned to any sacred frequency. Just noise.

Mara doesn't move. Her eyes scan him like a worried nurse over a patient who won't admit he's bleeding.

Lior stares at the ceiling. His breath slows, becomes too even. Like a man trying to stay perfectly still so the fracture doesn't spread.

"You're here," he whispers again, not to her—but to the shape of her.

She nods. "I didn't leave."

He turns his head slightly. Doesn't meet her gaze.

"I don't think you're fake," he says.

"But you don't think I'm real either."

He doesn't reply.

She reaches toward the Gospel on the floor. He jerks—violent.

"Don't," he says.

"I wasn't going to read it."

"Even proximity contaminates."

She pulls her hand back. "Lior... I'm here."

"Then prove it," he says, voice sharp.

She swallows. "How?"

He watches her chest rise and fall.

Then he says: "Touch me again."

She does.

Her hand on his. No magic. No glitch. No static.

Just skin.

But he doesn't sigh. Doesn't settle.

He closes his eyes, and behind them, Ashren whispers: "She cried. So did you. But only one of you bled."

Lior pulls away from her hand.

She waits.

When he finally rises, it's to retrieve the Gospel. He opens to a fresh page. Writes, without hesitation:

She screamed. So did I. But only one of us bled.

The ink smears at the edges.

He stares at the page for a long time.

Mara dresses silently behind him.

Before she leaves, she stops at the door. Doesn't turn.

"I hope you come back."

He doesn't answer.

The door closes with a sound too final.

Minutes pass.

Then a soft thunk beneath the door.

A letter.

Lior stares at it for what feels like hours.

Then bends. Opens.

Appointment confirmed: Dr. Ansel Mira. Thursday. 3:15 PM.

He doesn't remember booking it.

But he doesn't cancel.

12

Confronting the Divine

Lior stood on the edge of New Town, staring up at the façade of 117a Thistle Lane. Dr. Ansel Mira's office was nestled between a language therapy centre and a boutique selling nothing but grey, overpriced wool.

He hated it already.

He pushed the buzzer with a knuckle.

The door clicked.

No waiting room. No receptionist. Just one hallway, one door at the end—half-glass, blurred with frosted patterns like frost on a mirror.

He stepped inside.

It wasn't what he expected.

No couch. No desk. No sterile lighting. Just a circular room, painted in soft moss green, with two armchairs facing each other on a faded rug. A low table between them held a carafe of water, two glasses, a wooden bowl of smooth river stones. Light spilled through tall windows but didn't glare.

And Dr. Mira was already seated.

No lab coat. No stethoscope. No clipboard. Just a man in a navy jumper and dark jeans, hands folded loosely in his lap. His face was neither old nor young. The kind of face that had stopped aging years ago and simply... remained.

"Lior," he said, like a fact.

Lior sat stiffly, arms crossed.

He scanned the room. No cameras. No wires. But something about the stillness unnerved him more than surveillance would have.

"So," he started, tone clipped. "I guess you want me to explain."

Mira smiled faintly. "Only if you want to."

Lior watched him, waiting for the trap.

"I don't hear voices," Lior said, flatly.

"I didn't say you did."

"I've had... impressions. Feelings. Visitors."

"Visitors?"

"Not hallucinations." Sharper now. "Not delusions."

Mira nodded once. "Of course."

"They're not me."

"Then what are they?"

Lior's lips twitched. "Symbols. Alignments. It's not like a movie."

Mira leaned slightly forward, elbows resting on the arms of his chair. "Tell me how they love you."

That stopped Lior.

He blinked.

"...What?"

"You said they aren't you. So they must be something. How do they love you?"

He wasn't sure if it was a trap or the only honest question anyone had asked him in years.

"They protect," he said slowly. "They warn. They watch."

"Do they listen?"

Lior hesitated.

"...Sometimes."

"Do they wait for you to be ready?"

He didn't answer.

Mira sat back. "You don't have to prove they're real. You only need to ask if they trust you back."

The words settled like mist.

Lior stood abruptly. "That's enough for today."

Mira didn't flinch. "Same time next week?"

Lior paused. Didn't say yes. Didn't say no.

He left the room.

Behind him, the Gospel burned inside his coat like it had heard every word.

The streets of New Town stretched ahead in geometric patience—lines of orderly windows, clean-cut cornices, pavement unmarred by graffiti. It made Lior uneasy. Too controlled. Too quiet. Even the wind felt like it moved by instruction.

He walked with no direction, but the Gospel grew heavier against his side with each step. Not metaphorically—literally. The spine pressed harder against his ribs, as if burdened with warning.

He turned down a narrow lane, passed a parked delivery van, and the shadows turned cold.

That's when Thalos spoke.

"You let him open you."

Lior froze mid-step. The voice came from somewhere between his left ear and the third rib on his back.

"You let him taste the signal."

"Shut up," Lior muttered. "You're not in charge."

Another voice followed—slower, clinical, metallic.

Virel.

"Mira is calibration poison. Return to cycle. Reinstate the Pattern. Disruption breeds vulnerability."

Lior kept walking. Faster now.

But the city turned against him.

A man passed too close—his coat brushed Lior's shoulder. In the corner of his eye, the man's face blurred. Not fast. Not invisible. Just... off, like a sketch being redrawn.

Ashren bloomed behind his eyes. Cool and nostalgic.

"You know what they did last time you spoke," it whispered. "The white walls. The straps. The pills that slowed time. The room with no corners."

Lior nearly stumbled. His breath caught. The alley opened into a main road, noise cascading over him—bus brakes, a shouting teenager, a squealing stroller wheel.

Everyone stared too long.

Or didn't blink.

Or smiled just a moment after passing.

He ducked into a narrow stairwell. Concrete, wet from a leaky pipe above. The air smelled of rot and old takeaway wrappers. He pressed his back to the wall and slid down until he was sitting.

The Gospel wouldn't open. Its pages stuck. Like a mouth refusing to speak.

He thumbed the cover with trembling fingers. "You heard him. You know he saw me."

The pages didn't move.

He shook it. "Show me!"

Nothing.

He opened his coat. There, beneath his shirt, a faint ink-bruise: Selith's sigil, once ghostlike, now darkened. Warmer. Breathing.

He shut his eyes.

Voices flooded in.

Thalos: "Write until the truth cracks."

Virel: "Scrub the session from memory. Burn the transcript."

Ashren: "Remember the cage. It remembers you."

He covered his ears. They still echoed.

Finally, a new voice surfaced—not loud, not clear. Internal. His own, maybe.

"He is not your enemy."

Lior opened his eyes.

The city looked the same. But he didn't feel watched anymore.

He stood.

And the Gospel's spine clicked.

Like a lock unlatched.

The flat was dark when Lior returned—not by accident. He hadn't paid the power bill. Not because he couldn't. He just didn't want to. The dark was cleaner. Honest. The hum of electronics, the subtle frequencies they emitted, always felt too much lately.

But tonight, without it, the quiet was a skin he couldn't wear comfortably.

He sat on the floor beside the aquarium. The fish drifted behind the basalt tomb, their movements slow, disinterested in the world he'd shaped around them. Lior leaned his head back against the wall. The Gospel lay open in his lap, but the pages remained blank. Waiting. Punishing.

The phone rang.

He almost didn't answer.

But something—something low in the body, not the mind—made him reach.

He didn't check the screen. He just answered.

"Lior?" The voice was breath. Hesitant.

Mara.

His lips parted. He didn't speak.

"I just wanted to say..." she trailed off, but didn't hang up.

Silence sat between them for seven full seconds.

Then, softly: "I'm glad you answered."

Something in Lior broke.

Not violently. Not loudly. Just... broke.

A sound escaped his throat—not quite a sob. Not quite a word. Something raw.

She didn't ask what was wrong. She didn't ask anything.

She waited.

And he wept. Quietly. Bitterly.

Not from despair. Not even from fear.

But from *recognition*.

Because for the first time in weeks, a voice reached him that didn't try to rewrite his code.

It didn't demand. Or warn. Or twist memory.

It just stayed.

He wiped his face with his sleeve. The Gospel stirred, a page flipping on its own. He didn't look.

Instead, he spoke.

"I don't know who's real anymore."

Her voice held. "You are."

He swallowed. "I can't prove that."

"You don't have to."

They didn't say goodbye. The line just faded into silence.

Lior stared at the Gospel.

In the margin of the new page, in his own handwriting—but too precise to be recent—were the words:

Today the mirror blinked. And I saw myself on the other side.

He traced the sentence once. Then closed the book.

The sigil on his chest pulsed once, and faded.

That night, Lior didn't dream. Or if he did, he couldn't access it. The static didn't sing. The angels didn't argue. The walls didn't pulse with invisible sound.

There was just stillness.

He woke at 3:11 AM, the usual haunt. But the monitors didn't flicker.

The kettle didn't click. Even the fish were silent behind the basalt tomb, as if something sacred had been removed from the circuitry of the world.

He sat up. Rubbed his eyes. Waited.

Nothing.

He reached for the Gospel, but it wouldn't open. Not stuck, just... inert. Like a body no longer occupied.

He stood. Walked the flat. Touched the walls. Whispered names.

"Selith," he said, breath shallow.

No answer.

"Ozel."

Nothing.

"Thalos. Virel. Ashren."

No voice replied.

He went to the window. The city below was motionless in fog. Streetlights like ancient relics buried in mist. One gull, static as a model, hovered above a lamppost, wings spread unnaturally still.

He pressed his forehead to the glass.

And then—

A hum.

Not sound.

Pressure.

Behind him.

He turned slowly.

The Gospel had opened.

One page only. No symbols. Just words.

One sentence:

You are not unworthy of silence.

Lior sat on the floor.

He did not weep. Not this time.

He just nodded.

The sigil on his chest faded completely, leaving pale skin behind.

Unmarked. Unwritten.

He placed the Gospel back on the shelf. Not reverently. Not fearfully. Just gently.

Like closing the lid of something that had spoken long enough.

13

The Mirror cracks

Lior sat in the narrow chair by the window, not the couch. Always by the window. He liked the view—George Street curling off into a lane of trees, the clean trim of rooftops and spires. It made things feel possible, even if he didn't believe in possibility anymore.

Dr. Mira sat opposite. Same chair. Same mug. Always peppermint. No notepad. No pen. Just hands rested gently on the arms of the chair and that maddening, unshakable calm.

"So," Mira said, his voice the kind that didn't echo. "Have the voices been clearer this week?"

Lior's jaw flexed. "I wouldn't call them voices."

"What would you call them?"

He glanced out the window. A car stopped at the light, engine low and rhythmic like a purr. "Visitors," he said finally. "Advisors. Sometimes, I think they're echoes. Sometimes... I think they're me in a different configuration."

Mira didn't nod or smile. Just: "And when they disagree?"

"They always disagree," Lior said. "That's how I know they're real."

Mira leaned back slightly. "Do you trust them?"

That question stuck. Lior blinked, as if trying to load the answer from somewhere far away. "I used to," he said.

Silence. Clean. No weight. Mira never rushed him.

Eventually, Mira asked, "Do you have the notebook with you today?"

Lior's hand was already resting on his bag. His fingers tensed.

"The Gospel," Mira added, softly. "Would you read me a page?"

Lior met his gaze. Not defiant. Just... measured.

"It's not ready."

"No?"

"It's too volatile. If you heard it now, it might undo something."

"I see," Mira said. "Then you're protecting me."

Lior looked down, unsure whether to feel insulted or seen.

"I'll ask again next week," Mira said, without threat.

That was the end of it.

—-

Back on the street, Lior walked slower than usual. His pace didn't match the traffic. He stopped at the intersection one second too late. Crossed on the fourth flicker. Disordered.

The Gospel burned in his bag.

But he didn't open it.

Not yet.

Lior left the flat that morning at exactly 9:17, as instructed.

That was Virel's number—9:17 meant alignment with pedestrian crossing cycles. Protection via grid sync. A day encoded for clarity.

Except... he paused at the door. Hand on the knob. Air in his lungs. Something in him buckled.

What if he left at 9:18?

He waited.

The seconds passed like stones dragged through water. The clock flipped. 9:18.

He turned the knob.

The air outside didn't shift. No ripple in the street. No honk. No scream. No angel tearing through his skull.

Just Edinburgh. Wet. Quiet. Complicit.

He walked.

Thalos whispered in his left ear, sharp and certain: "Now you'll see."

But he didn't. Nothing happened.

The bus still passed. The girl in the yellow coat still crossed his path. The same poster peeled on the same lamp post. The rhythm of reality stuttered—but did not collapse.

He tried again at the crosswalk.

Virel said: "Wait for the fifth flicker."

He crossed on the third.

No crash. No warning. No divine course correction.

Just a man walking against the light.

He opened The Gospel on a bench, breath shallow.

It was a mess.

Symbols overlaid symbols. Lines through previous lines. Not corrections—rejections. Pages warped from too many redraws, too many inks. Paper torn from being pressed too hard.

Virel's voice returned later that afternoon.

"Remove page sixteen. Burn it."

Lior opened to page sixteen.

It was blank.

He didn't burn it.

He drew a square around it. Labeled it: False command.

That night, Ozel appeared again.

In the bathroom mirror. Daylight behind it.

Lior stared. The face was too long. The eyes too close. Smiling, but the lips never moved.

"Tell me you're real," Lior whispered.

Ozel leaned forward.

So did his reflection.

And then the reflection spoke—not aloud, but in thought:

You don't want real. You want meaningful.

Lior stepped back.

The mirror didn't.

It stayed close.

—-

He didn't sleep that night. The Gospel pulsed with phantom lines.

The choir of angels had lost its harmony.

And silence now sounded like betrayal.
—-

Dr. Mira didn't ask questions the way most therapists did.

He didn't say "tell me about your childhood," or "what do you think that means?"

He said, "Let's look at the perimeter. Where do your memories begin to blur?"

Lior answered without thinking.

"There's a hallway. Narrow. Brown carpet. My mother's voice. She's crying."

Mira nodded, didn't speak.

"I can't see her face. Just her back. She's crouched. Or maybe kneeling. There's light coming in from the door. Morning, I think. Maybe afternoon. She says my name. She says it soft."

"What's on the walls?" Mira asked.

Lior blinked.

"What?"

"In the hallway. Are there frames? Pictures? Wallpaper?"

Lior's mouth moved, but no sound came out. He frowned.

"I don't know."

"And what happens next?" Mira asked, gently.

"I... don't remember. I just know she was sad. I was scared."

Mira's head tilted, slow as water tipping in a glass. "Do you remember your body in the scene? Are you looking through your own eyes?"

Lior's spine chilled. "No."

He rubbed his temples.

"No, I'm watching it. From behind. From above."

"And how old were you?"

"Twelve? Maybe seven. I don't—"

The Gospel flashed behind his eyes. A page with no date. A scene described in ink and fire. A symbol drawn beneath the line: Mother's grief is the origin point.

Lior's voice cracked. "It's not real, is it?"

Mira didn't confirm. He didn't deny.

He simply said, "Sometimes we inherit images like we inherit scars. They aren't always ours to own."

Lior stood abruptly.

The walls of the office felt too close. The room hummed faintly—he was sure the vent in the ceiling had never made that sound before.

"Then whose memory is it?" he snapped.

Mira folded his hands. "Perhaps the question is... who benefits from you believing it?"

— -

Later, Lior stared at the Gospel.

That scene. That hallway. It was there—drawn three times. Once in color pencil. Once in ash. Once in reversed ink.

He took a razor blade.

Cut them out.

The pages bled just slightly.
  The instruction was clear:

"Turn left at the corner. Do not pause. Do not look into the florist window."

Thalos had spoken it in the old tone—the one wrapped in thunder and certainty.

But Lior was tired.

Tired of listening. Tired of obeying. Tired of fearing punishment that never came.

So he turned right.

The sky did not darken.

No thunder cracked the air.

A delivery truck rolled by, low and rattling. A child shouted across the street. A bus pulled into a stop and waited. The florist window reflected only glass and sunlight.

And Lior stood frozen, breath shallow.

Nothing happened.

No collapse. No curse. No angel fell screaming from the clouds.

His heart beat unevenly. He opened his coat. The Gospel was still there. Still warm. But when he unwrapped it, the ink shimmered wrong. Letters swam. Diagrams shifted mid-line. Pages clung to each other like damp skin.

He turned to the last entry Thalos had dictated.

It read:

"Turn left at the corner. Do not pause. Do not look into the florist window."

Then beneath it, hastily scrawled—by a different hand?

"The command has no teeth. The light bends because you believe it must."

Lior stared. The handwriting was tighter. Taller. And it was written in black ink he didn't own.

He slammed the Gospel shut.

The city seemed to hiccup.

Not shake. Not move. But hesitate. One of the pigeons on the roof across the street flapped once, hovered in place, then resumed its arc—as if the frames had skipped.

Lior stumbled home.

He ripped open the Gospel and wrote over pages. Scribbles over sigils. Crossed-out sermons. Arrows pointing nowhere.

He muttered aloud, not to the angels, but to himself:

"You lied."

"You needed me afraid."

"You needed me obedient."

Each phrase written like penance. Like confession. Like war.

The Gospel bled through. Pages curled. The binding crackled under strain.

And from somewhere deep in its spine, a whisper—not one of the known voices.

Something deeper.

Older.

It said:

"Even your rebellion follows design."
  —-

The Gospel no longer hums. It breathes.

Lior walks New Town with it clutched under his coat, the shape of it pressing against his ribs like a bruise. The text has bled through every page. Layered scripts, overwritten diagrams, corners torn from rewriting paths that never led where they promised.

He doesn't know where he's going.

His feet drag him across tram lines, down alleyways where the geometry feels wrong. Pavement tiles that alternate unevenly. Windows too narrow, too tall.

The air has weight.

The silence of the city is broken only by whispers he can't isolate. Thalos repeats the same phrase, louder each time: "Re-alignment is critical." Virel mutters numbers that don't resolve. Ashren breathes childhood lullabies backward. Ozel hums from the mouth of a sewer drain.

Selith is silent.

The one he trusted. The one who never forced.

Gone.

He clutches the Gospel tighter. It is warm. Too warm. Like it's feeding on him.

A child on a passing bus points at him. Laughs. Her teeth are all wrong— vertical rows, like tally marks.

Lior breaks into a run.

He doesn't know how long he moves—only that when he stops, he's outside a charity shop. A storefront of thick glass and mannequin torsos dressed in church blazers.

He's breathing hard.

Then he sees it.

His reflection.

And behind him—five figures.

Each one still. Each haloed with light that shouldn't be. Not cast, but absorbed.

Their eyes are not eyes. Just shapes. Darker than the reflections should allow.

He turns.

There is no one behind him.

He looks again.

Still there.

One of them lifts its hand. Waves.

Lior drops the Gospel.

The sound it makes against the pavement is wet. Not paper. Not leather.

Wet.

He doesn't pick it up.

He runs.

Full sprint, into the crowd, into a world that suddenly seems too loud, too bright, too incorrect.

Inside the glass behind him, the five figures do not move.

They do not need to.

They have already entered him.

14

The Silence

It happens like breath held too long. The first to go is Thalos. Mid-sentence, mid-warning—his voice simply... cuts. No final command. No tapering echo. Just an unfinished word and then silence.

Lior blinks. Waits. Nothing.

He sets his pencil down, spine tightening. The room feels heavier, not empty but thick—like a stage after the actors have left, and the lights stay on too long.

He listens harder.

But Virel doesn't speak either. No countdowns. No metric reminders. No "left foot first" or "face north to sip." The metronome in Lior's head clicks once, then falls silent.

He checks the Gospel. The sigils stare back at him, inert. The lines no longer shimmer.

"Selith?" he says aloud, almost a whisper. His own voice sounds strange. Loud. Alone.

He turns to the mirror above the sink—where Ozel has appeared before, edges twitching.

Nothing.

Just his face. Pale. Tired. Unaccompanied.

He walks the flat slowly, checking corners, testing routines. He flicks the lights off, then on. Nothing. Opens the fridge, takes out a piece of bread, breaks it in half. Waits for a signal.

None comes.

He leaves the kettle boiling too long, hoping Virel will scold him. Hoping for that familiar pressure in his chest. But only the rising screech of steam.

He stares at the empty room.

The absence becomes unbearable in layers—because it's not just quiet. It's too quiet. Not peaceful.

It's a vacuum. A missing limb. An amputated frequency.

He sits on the floor. Tries humming the tone Selith used to lull him. It catches in his throat. Turns to a cough. Then dry silence.

He clutches The Gospel to his chest like a relic from a dead god.

In the stillness, he murmurs to no one:

"Where did you go?"

No answer.

Only the tick of the wall clock, slow and indifferent.

He opens it with ceremony, expecting ritual.

The Gospel rests on the desk, but it feels cold. Lifeless. No longer the breathing text it used to be. The pages don't ripple when he flips them. No more invisible drafts waiting in the margins. No more glyphs sketching themselves.

He scans them with growing unease.

The loops are still there. The symbols. The spirals. But the meaning is gone. It's like reading someone else's dream in a language he used to understand but has now forgotten.

He reads a sentence aloud:

Z-lock: measure from marrow to mirror.

Nothing happens.

He tries another:

If you hear the train twice, turn the stairs into silence.

Still nothing.

He slams the cover shut.

It makes a hollow sound.

His hands shake—not with fear, but with betrayal. He tears a page out. The corner rips jagged. The spiral bleeds to the edge. He holds it in front of the desk lamp, tilting it like an ancient map.

It says nothing.

Another page—this one blackened with charcoal lines and red pen swipes. He doesn't remember drawing it, but it's in his hand, and that makes it his. He stares at it until the lines blur.

Then, slowly, he crumples it.

The paper crunches with too much finality.

He lights a candle. Watches the flame. Feeds the page into it. The fire eats it hungrily. The ashes curl and fall without resistance.

Still nothing.

Another page. Then another. Then five.

The Gospel thins.

He rips until he's surrounded by a graveyard of pages, his breath shallow, his face lit only by the flickering candlelight and the fractured images of diagrams once sacred.

The Gospel, once alive, is now a body.

And he?

He is its killer.

He stares at the spine of it. Bent. Naked.

And for the first time, thinks:

Maybe it was never speaking.

Maybe it was always him.

And that thought cuts sharper than the silence.
   The door clicks behind him. The lock sounds mechanical now. Not divine. Just a lock. Just a door.

Lior steps into the street with no compass, no alignment, no signal. The sky is too bright. The colours too honest. His breath fogs slightly in the morning air, but it's not the breath of prophecy—it's just condensation.

Everything has lost its veil.

The first person he sees is an old woman dragging a tartan cart. Her shoe is untied. He doesn't feel a pattern in it. He only sees a tripping hazard. He doesn't warn her.

A man jogs past, earbuds in, sweat soaking his neckline. Lior doesn't try to decode his pace.

A child drops a toy. Lior doesn't flinch. The toy isn't a symbol. It's just plastic. Blue.

He walks.

Everywhere, he sees things for what they are.

The brickwork doesn't rhyme.

The graffiti is just swears.

No lampposts hum. No gutters align. No pigeons form sigils.

Everything is suddenly, violently itself.

At first, he's numb. Then something colder blooms in his chest.

Exile.

The angels weren't guides.

They were filters.

And now he walks Edinburgh raw. Every noise too real. Every scent uncurated. Every movement unshielded. The coffee shop windows reflect only his face now, not his shadow companions.

He walks past his usual café. Mara isn't there. He doesn't check.

He passes Waverley. Doesn't count the tiles.

He stops at Princes Street Gardens. There's a dead pigeon near the fountain. Wings awkward, eyes glassy. Nothing poetic. Just death.

He sits on the nearest bench.

Not cross-legged. Not aligned. Just human.

The city presses in around him. He doesn't cry. That would feel too much like punctuation.

Instead, he stares at the bird. And thinks:

It didn't die to say anything.

And that thought is heavier than scripture.
  The bench creaks. He doesn't look up.

Soft steps. Slow approach. A shape in his periphery. Then stillness. The presence doesn't move away. Doesn't say his name. Doesn't make a sound.

She just sits beside him.

Mara.

The wind cuts through the trees, stirring leaves that have already fallen. The pigeon lies untouched.

Lior doesn't speak.

Neither does she.

Minutes pass.

A siren wails far off. A car backfires. Someone laughs too loud. A dog barks three times. Lior hears it all.

But not Mara.

She breathes slowly, shoulders still.

Finally, he speaks. Not to her, not to anyone, just into the air:

"I thought they were protecting me."

Mara says nothing.

He swallows. Continues.

"I thought they were... leading me somewhere. That it all meant something."

She shifts slightly. Not toward him. Not away.

He glances down. Her hand rests on the bench, palm up.

Open.

Not offering. Not demanding.

Just there.

He doesn't take it. But he sees it.

His throat aches from silence. Not imposed, but chosen.

Mara finally speaks.

Just one word.

"Okay."

And somehow, that single syllable feels heavier than all the whispers combined.

He closes his eyes.

They sit like that. The dead pigeon still between them. The world still unfiltered.

And for the first time since it all began, he doesn't want the voices back.

He just wants to sit.

Not know.

Just be.

The office is too quiet. It always has been, but today, it presses differently. No internal murmur, no divine hum. Just the faint buzz of city life bleeding through soundproofed walls.

Dr. Mira waits. Not impatient. Not prodding. Just present.

Lior stands in the doorway longer than necessary. Holding it. Holding everything.

He steps in.

The Gospel is under his arm. Looser than before. As if the book itself has lost weight.

He doesn't sit right away. Instead, he approaches Mira's desk, rests the notebook on its surface, and runs his fingers along the cover's edge.

"I burned a page," he says.

Mira doesn't flinch. "Did it help?"

Lior shrugs. "It didn't scream."

That lands in the space between them like a dropped stone.

Then, after a breath:

"I think I need to know what's mine," Lior says, his voice barely audible.

Mira nods once. "Will you read to me?"

Lior opens the Gospel.

The pages no longer glow. No shimmer, no whisper beneath the ink. Just words. Jagged, overwritten, layered with madness—but his.

He clears his throat.

Reads aloud.

It's not graceful. It's not coherent. Some lines are half-written in static, others in spirals, some in tongues he no longer understands. But he reads them all.

He stumbles. Winces. Skips nothing.

And Mira listens.

Not analyzing. Not decoding.

Just listening.

When Lior finishes, he closes the book slowly. Looks up.

"I don't know what any of that meant."

Mira leans forward.

"Maybe it wasn't about meaning."

Lior nods. Silent.

The Gospel feels heavier now.

But in the right way.

He leaves the office without it.

For the first time, he walks into the street empty-handed.

And whole.

15

The Awakening

Lior sat rigid in the old leather chair, its cracked arms warm from the afternoon sun. Across from him, Dr. Mira folded his hands, not over a notepad, not behind a screen, just calmly in his lap—waiting. The office was quiet. No humming machines. No tick of a clock. Only the low creak of the building's bones when the wind moved.

On the table between them, Lior placed The Gospel. He hadn't touched it in three days.

Mira gestured gently. "Whenever you're ready."

Lior nodded. His fingers hovered over the cover for a moment, uncertain if it would resist him, or open itself like before. But this time, it was just a book. His hands shook as he flipped past pages smeared with old graphite, warped with spilled tea, marked with symbols even he no longer understood.

He began to read aloud.

At first, his voice caught on the edges of the words. The syllables were strange—half-poetry, half-instruction. He read a passage meant to align stair steps with lunar cycles, and paused. Mira didn't flinch. He kept going.

Some pages carried beauty:
"The sky folds inward when I'm right. Mara's eyes align with doorways."

Some were terrifying:
"If I speak aloud at 2:16, the windows will shatter—only spiritually, but real enough to scar."

Others made no sense at all:
*"Left. Left. Circle. Salt. Seven."

He turned a page and flinched at what he saw—one whole section blacked out with ink, angrily. Beneath the smudges, faint shapes still whispered themselves into form. He skipped it. Kept reading.

His voice steadied, strangely. There was a rhythm buried inside him, not divine now, but muscle memory. A lifetime of being haunted transmuted into story.

Then came the names.

Lior's lips faltered. Names he didn't recognize. Dozens of them. Maybe people. Maybe places. Maybe neither.

He kept reading.

Then the symbols. Diagrams of windows. Circles within squares. A shape he once thought was a sigil but now just looked like a doodle drawn under pressure.

Mira hadn't said a word.

Lior kept reading.

And finally—he reached the end.

The final page.

It wasn't elaborate. No grand glyph. No final prophecy.

Just a sentence. Scrawled in a shaky, uneven hand. Not his usual script. Something younger. More frightened.

"Tell me what to believe now."

The words hung in the room like smoke.

Lior closed the book. Not with reverence, but with resignation. He stared at the cover, then at Mira.

Dr. Mira's voice was soft. No trace of judgment.

"You've already begun to ask."

Lior breathed.

And for the first time in months, no voice answered him back.

Lior stepped into the street like someone emerging from underwater. The wind on Queen Street hit his face sharp and clean, and for a moment he swayed—disoriented not by dizziness, but by stillness. No static. No voice tracing instructions into the corners of his vision. Just the ordinary world, breathing its ordinary rhythms.

He walked without ritual. No counted steps. No mapped shadows. His body wanted to revert, to look for symmetry in the bricks or signal in the shop signs. But he didn't follow it. He let himself be... unpatterned.

Back at his flat, he unlocked the door without hesitation. No angels hovered by the hinges. No tremor of divine code in the threshold.

The Gospel sat on the desk. He did not touch it.

Instead, he picked up a fresh notebook—one with blank pages, wide-ruled, soft cream. It had no name yet. No sigils marked its spine. Just a cheap corner-store brand and a thin graphite pencil he'd sharpened down to a toothpick.

He opened it. Wrote, slowly:

"I liked the way Mara looked at me when I told her about the wind."

The sentence sat there like a loose thread on the edge of a sweater. It didn't pull toward madness. It didn't summon any whisper from beyond.

It was just... a thought.

He flipped the page. Wrote another:

"Maybe I was not chosen. Maybe I am just alive."

That one hurt more. Like pulling a splinter he didn't know was embedded under his ribs.

He kept writing:

"I like the way coffee smells even when I don't want to drink it."

"I want to hear what Davin sounds like when he's not afraid of me."

"I don't think I loved Selith. I think I loved being needed."

When he paused, the room was silent.

Not empty. Just silent.

He looked at the Gospel.

Then shelved it.

Not discarded. Not destroyed.

Just... finished.

He didn't cleanse it. Didn't bless it. Didn't wrap it in salt or wire or place a protection stone atop it.

He shelved it the way he shelved other past notebooks—ones filled with sketches and class notes and grocery lists.

The Grand Year had ended.

He turned back to his new notebook. Picked up the pencil again.

Wrote one last line before bed:

"There is more to me than what watched me."
   The city moved around him again, and this time Lior let it.

No decoding.

No tracing of angles.

He stood at a corner on Nicolson Street and waited for the crosswalk light without scanning the patterns in the blinking countdown. Just waited. And when it flashed green, he walked.

The shops were still strange. The windows still held reflections that once seemed deeper than glass. But now he looked into them and saw a man—not a prophet, not a vessel. Just himself.

He met a woman's gaze as she passed him, a stranger with tired eyes and a bag of groceries. She didn't avert her eyes. Neither did he. That was all.

He bought toothpaste. Paid in exact change. The coins felt human in his palm. He remembered how they clinked when he was a child, dropping them into an arcade machine. That memory was real. Entirely his.

Back home, he unpacked nothing sacred. Just necessities. He opened a new tab on his browser and searched for poetry magazines—not to decode them. To help them.

He answered an email. Designed a clean homepage. Pale blues. Elegant serif font. No sigils. No sigil hidden in the margins. No secret instructions encoded in line height or padding.

He wrote the alt-text clearly: "Title banner. Image of waves. Accessible font."

And for the first time in months, he hit "send" without fear.

Later, he cleaned. Not obsessively. Not according to a ritual. Just swept the floor. Washed a dish. Folded his shirt.

The kettle clicked when the water was ready. He made tea. It steeped too long. He didn't care.

That night, as he settled onto the couch with his new notebook, he noticed something in the quiet.

Not a voice.

Not a whisper.

Just space.

He wrote:

"I don't want to be sacred. I want to be kind."

He looked at the sentence.

It did not vibrate.

It did not shift.

It stayed.

And so did he.
   It took time before he trusted the quiet.

At first, he flinched at small sounds—the hum of the fridge, the soft buzz of streetlights. His mind waited for the shift, the message, the twist. But it never came.

He watched television without hearing voices layered in the static. Commercials played and ended. Sitcoms had laugh tracks. Nothing divine interrupted.

The Gospel remained shelved, spine outward, beside an old sketchbook and a copy of House of Leaves he never finished. He didn't touch it. Didn't need to.

He walked through Edinburgh now not as a disciple, but as a man. He noticed things still—cracked stones, uneven signage—but they were just things. Imperfect. Real.

In Princes Street Gardens, he sat without intention. No diagrams. No notes. Just watched children feed pigeons. Watched couples argue, then make up. Watched a man nap on a bench, arms crossed like he owned the world.

No one watched him.

He was no longer the center of anything.

The absence felt, at first, like loneliness. But it wasn't. It was... a return. To himself. To a world uninterpreted.

One evening, he heard a knock. Just once.

Mara stood there. She didn't say, "I was worried." Didn't say, "I missed you." She simply asked:

"Want to walk?"

They did. Side by side. Past the Water of Leith, beneath the bridges that once whispered. Now, they echoed only their footsteps.

They didn't speak. Not much.

When they did, it wasn't about angels or codes or patterns.

He said, "I tried to control everything. Even the mystery."

She said, "You were scared."

He nodded. "Still am."

She took his hand.

He let her.

Later, he wrote in his new notebook:

"There is a silence that is not absence. It is permission."

He closed the book without needing to underline it.

The flat was still.

No static.

No watchers.

Just a window cracked open, and the wind—ordinary, unscripted—moving through it.
    A week passes.

Then another.

No voices. No visions. No rituals. No breaking points.

Lior drinks tea without counting sips. Lets toast burn slightly. Misses a bin shot and doesn't correct it. It all happens without consequence.

On Sunday, he finds himself standing at the edge of the Meadows, watching people fly kites. He smiles at one shaped like a squid. The wind pulls it sharp against the sky, its long red tails writhing in the air like it's dancing with no one watching.

He opens his notebook on a nearby bench and writes:

"I no longer need to be deciphered."

He underlines it. Once. That's enough.

He walks past a church that used to radiate tension. Now, it's just stone and stained glass. Inside, a choir sings. He doesn't understand the language. That's okay.

He steps in. Sits in the back.

Just listens.

When it ends, he exits. Quiet. Whole.

That night, he opens The Gospel. Just once. Flips to the last filled page. Doesn't read it. Just tears it out slowly.

He places it in the bin. Gently.

Then, with clean hands, he opens his new notebook.

The first page still reads:

"I liked the way Mara looked at me when I told her about the wind."

On the next, he writes:

"In silence, I am nothing. In madness, I was someone. In this... I am becoming."

He closes the notebook.

Turns off the light.

And sleeps.

16

Rebuilding Bridges

The pub is small, old, half-sunk into the cobbles. It smells of wood polish and burnt bread. The kind of place that's never full, never loud, and never changes hands.

Lior arrives early—earlier than he should have. Not to prepare, but because waiting feels less frightening than arriving late. He sits near the back, under a slanted beam and a faded painting of a stag. The wood creaks around him. His hands are still. That surprises him.

Mara enters like she always does: unannounced, inevitable. Her coat is unbuttoned. Her eyes sweep the room once, land on him. She smiles. No hesitation. Just... walks over.

She orders wine at the bar. Then joins him without a word. Sits opposite. Shrugs off her coat. Her hair is longer. Maybe softer.

He waits for the voices. The layers. The static. But nothing comes.

Just her.

She sips. Then looks at him properly. "You look... like you've been sleeping."

"I have," he says. It feels almost like a lie.

A pause. Then: "You haven't seen me in weeks."

"I know."

"I thought you were gone."

"I was."

Another silence, this one not empty but full—of what wasn't said during those weeks, of what could have broken instead of bent.

"I'm sorry I didn't trust you," he says.

She doesn't blink. Doesn't fold inward. Just lifts her chin slightly. "You didn't know how."

He nods.

They sit like that a while. Not quite talking. Not quite drifting.

And for the first time in a long time, he isn't scanning her for signs. Doesn't interpret the tilt of her glass, the pattern of her earrings. She is just Mara. Real. Present. Without metaphor.

She finishes her wine. Doesn't ask for another. "Let's walk?"

He stands.

And the city doesn't whisper when they step outside.
  The message was short. Just five words:
  I want to talk. - L

He didn't expect a reply. But Davin sent one three minutes later.
  Come to the house. I'll be there.

The house is the same. Their parents' place. Neutral ground. A shell of echoing stairs and old rugs that never quite lost their shape. Lior arrives second. Davin's car is already in the drive.

He knocks once, then lets himself in. No need to pretend formality.

Davin is in the kitchen, two mugs on the counter. One already steaming.

"You still drink black?" he asks without turning.

Lior nods. "Yeah."

They sit across from each other at the small table, the one that still has a burn mark from when Lior left a candle too long as a teenager. Neither of them mentions it.

"I thought maybe you'd..." Davin starts, then stops.

Lior finishes for him. "Snapped?"

"Yeah. Or disappeared. I don't know."

"I did. Sort of."

They sip. The silence that follows is neither awkward nor tense. Just weighted. Like both know not everything has to be said to be understood.

"I saw the pages," Davin says eventually. "What you wrote. What you drew."

Lior looks down. "You think I was crazy?"

"I think you were... drowning. But you swam weird."

Lior laughs. It's small, surprised. Honest.

"You scared me," Davin adds. "Not because of what you believed. But because you stopped looking at me like I was real."

That hits harder than any angel's whisper. Lior breathes in slowly, like it hurts.

"I didn't know how to come back."

"You're here now."

They don't hug. Don't cry. They just sit. Drink. Exist.

Later, they walk the neighborhood. The pavement is uneven in places, the trees taller. A woman walks past with a stroller. A dog barks somewhere far off.

"I didn't think you'd reply," Lior says.

Davin shrugs. "You're my brother. You get chances."

They don't need more words than that.

The walk ends with a shared look. No promises. Just recognition.

And sometimes, that's enough.
Lior's workspace is quieter now.

Not silent—the city still hums beyond the windows, the radiator knocks occasionally, his tea cools beside the monitor—but inside his mind, the angels no longer dictate.

The Gospel sits shelved. High up. Dust starting to gather.

Today's task: a web layout for a small poetry magazine. The brief is simple—pastels, serif fonts, a clean structure that invites breath, not compression.

There's no instruction from Thalos. No "correct" placement whispered by Virel. No symbols clawing into the margins.

He begins with white.

Then, a soft blue—lavender with a grey undertone. A heading in dark ink, not black, but near it. The body font flows like something half-remembered.

He arranges the images. Edits the alignment. It takes him longer than it should—not because he's lost, but because he checks with himself now. There's no divine rhythm. Just instinct. Taste.

At one point, he pauses. Fingers hovering above the mouse.

A diagonal line in the banner feels wrong.

Not cursed. Not unclean.

Just... unkind to the eye.

He shifts it. By a degree. Then another. It falls into place—not because it means something. Because it feels right.

He exhales.

For the first time in months, he completes a layout and doesn't annotate it. Doesn't overlay glyphs or build sigils in negative space. He doesn't hide anything.

He prints a mock-up. Pins it to the wall. Stares at it.

It is simple.

It is good.

Later, at his next session, he brings the design to Dr. Mira.

"This doesn't mean anything," he says, a little uncertain, a little defensive.

Mira looks at it, then at him. Smiles, quietly.

"That's the beauty of it."

And something inside Lior—that once twisted thing hungry for patterns, divine signs, secret maps—unclenches just a little.

He walks home without checking the spacing of pavement tiles.

That night, he dreams of nothing.

And wakes up rested.

The apartment is no longer a sanctum.

There are no sigils taped to the walls. No salt lines near the windows. The closet has been cleared of notebooks, strings, graphite shavings. The tomb—aquarium turned altar—has gone dark. The basalt lies clean, dry. Ordinary.

Lior moves through the space differently now.

He opens drawers without dread. Touches surfaces without expecting a hum. The desk lamp flicks on with a simple click—no ritual, no invocation.

The static has gone.

Not banished. Not exorcised. Simply... left.

He finds himself listening for it anyway. At night. In the silence between breaths. In the hum of the fridge. In the low hiss of streetlights through the window.

But nothing comes.

One evening, he opens his new notebook and writes:

I miss them sometimes. But I do not want them back.

It startles him to see the sentence laid out so plainly. But it feels true. Not profound. Not sacred.

Just true.

He walks the streets without checking symbols. Crosses intersections without counting lights. A man offers him a flyer for a street performance; he takes it without suspicion. A stranger compliments his coat; he says thank you.

He doesn't feel holy.

But he doesn't feel haunted either.

Mara messages: Want to get coffee again? No weirdness this time. Just coffee.

He types back: Sounds good. I'll bring the awkward silences.

She sends a laughing emoji.

He smiles.

Later, standing at the window, he watches the city breathe. No loops. No fractures. Just movement. Life.

The air feels uncoiled.

He doesn't reach for The Gospel.

Instead, he lets his hand rest on the table.

Nothing moves beneath it.

And in that stillness, he feels not alone—but present.

Lior sits at the desk, elbows resting on a clean surface. No open notebooks. No humming screens. Just a blank page and a pen with no name.

He begins to write—not to channel, not to decipher. Just to say something.

"I liked the way Mara looked at me when I told her about the wind."

The sentence looks foreign in its simplicity. It doesn't loop. It doesn't encode.

It just speaks.

He closes the notebook and walks outside.

It's raining, soft and even. The kind of rain that doesn't chase you indoors. He leaves the umbrella at home. Edinburgh smells like wet earth and stone and a little bit of rust. Familiar.

He walks past the old café. Through the park. Past the shop where he first saw the wrong reflections.

This time, the glass shows only one figure. No angels. No static. Just him.

He arrives early at the pub near Grassmarket. Orders a drink. Sits by the window.

Mara enters ten minutes later, shaking off her coat. She smiles before she even reaches the table.

"Hi," she says.

"Hi."

They talk. Not about the past. Not about angels or spirals or divine scripts. They talk about books, about old films, about how weird it is when a seagull stares at you too long.

Lior laughs.

Not because he's being polite. But because he wants to.

Later, she says, "You seem… lighter."

He shrugs. "Still here. Just quieter inside."

She nods.

He walks her to her bus stop. When she leaves, she touches his hand.

Not a test. Not a ritual.

Just contact.

He walks home with a strange ache in his chest. Not grief. Not ecstasy.

Something new.

That night, he opens the notebook again. Writes one more sentence:

Maybe I was not chosen. Maybe I am just alive.

He doesn't try to explain it.

He just lets the ink dry.

17

The Fading Echoes

He wakes slowly.

No whispers. No humming. No pressure against his temples. Just the muted pulse of morning light pressing gently through the curtains.

The room is still. The kind of still that doesn't feel suspicious.

He lies there for a while, his cheek warm against the pillow. He listens—not for voices, but for birds, for the dull buzz of the city. Someone below his window starts a car. The kettle clicks on in the kitchen, automated. A small joy.

He doesn't reach for The Gospel. It's not beside the bed anymore.

He gets up. Pads barefoot to the kitchen. The air is cool, a little damp. He opens a fresh box of green tea, no ritual. No angles. Just a choice.

The tea steeps. He leans against the counter, watching the slow swirl of color bloom into the water. He used to believe the swirl meant something. Now he watches it just to watch.

At the desk, his email pings. A client from months ago—the one with the poetry site—has approved the last set of changes. They love it. They want to send a small bonus. He reads the message twice.

He replies: "Thank you. I'm glad it resonated."

Then he sits back and smiles.

He checks his phone. A message from Mara.

MARA: Saw a woman today with your hair. She looked haunted but cute. Made me think of you.

He laughs. Texts back: That's the dream, isn't it?

Then, after a pause: Thanks for remembering me.

The reply comes fast.

MARA: I never forgot. I just waited.

Later that afternoon, Mira's office feels brighter. Not different. Just noticed.

Mira sips something herbal. No clipboard. Just a couch and a chair and the small, watchful calm of someone who doesn't fill silence.

Lior talks easily now. About nothing in particular. Weather. Fonts. The weird way traffic patterns feel like breath. Mira listens.

Then asks: "Lior, what were the angels to you, really?"

Lior looks out the window for a long time.

Then he answers: "Parts of me. Trying to keep me safe. In a language I didn't speak yet."

Mira nods once. "That sounds like healing."

Lior doesn't reply.

He just feels the warmth of the tea cup in his hands.
   The flat smells like cinnamon dust and radiator heat.

He's pulling winter things from storage—scarves, an old jumper, gloves missing their pair—when he finds the jacket. Heavy. Blue. Thicker than he remembers. A relic of the year before The Gospel truly began to speak.

He checks the pockets automatically, hoping for a forgotten receipt or a lost fiver.

Instead, he finds a folded page.

Worn. Torn on one side. It's not his handwriting—except it is. Or was.

The ink is smudged at the corners. But the phrase at the top is clear:

Ashren: age eight, the candle with the dragon wick.

He feels his stomach clench. That birthday never happened. Not really.

He never had a dragon-shaped candle. His mother never made that cake. He never sat at the garden table with someone singing in a voice too deep to be hers.

Ashren invented that moment. Or borrowed it. Or stitched it to him.

Still, Lior reads the page. Every line. Every beat of nostalgia, even the manufactured bits.

He reads it once.

Then again.

The third time, his voice joins the words. Soft. Almost reverent.

Not because he believes them.

Because he remembers what it felt like to.

There is no tremble in his hands. No heat at the base of his neck. No static behind the eyes.

Only weight. Familiar. Manageable.

He sits at the desk, Gospel shelved above. He doesn't take it down.

Instead, he folds the page with care. Sharp corners. Clean lines.

He opens the drawer beside his bed and places it in.

Not hidden.

Not displayed.

Just... remembered.

A token.

A story once believed.

He touches the drawer lightly, lets his fingers rest against the wood.

Not to summon.

To honor.

Then he stands.

Crosses the room.

And turns on music.

Not static. Not hum.

Just a guitar. A voice. A song with no messages tucked between chords.

It plays softly.

And he lets it.
  It begins with light—thin and honeyed, slipping between clouds like forgiveness.

Lior walks alone. Grassmarket behind him, the castle outlined in shadow. No one follows. No symbols tug at the edges of things. The shops are closed. The shutters calm.

The city is still.

It breathes. And he breathes with it.

His steps echo—soft, not reverent. No rhythm imposed. No numbers counted. Just steps. Forward. A little uneven. Human.

Wind brushes his collar. Cold, but not invasive. He doesn't flinch.

His hands are in his pockets. His jaw loose. His eyes soft.

He walks past the café. The lights are off. Chairs upended on tables. The window reflects him, and nothing else.

No angels at his shoulder.

No Ozel behind the glass.

He turns up Victoria Street. The curve is familiar, but tonight, it doesn't feel like a loop or a symbol. Just a street. Just stone.

The sky shifts from gold to pearl. A slow descent of light.

Lior stops beneath a streetlamp. It flickers—once. He doesn't flinch. He doesn't interpret.

He just smiles.

The lamplight casts no shadows behind him.

Only forward.

He breathes in the quiet. Lets it fill him. Not like faith, not like madness. Just like breath.

And in that breath, he is whole.

***

He wakes.

The ceiling is familiar. The fan is off. The room is still.

His cheeks are damp. He doesn't wipe them. Not yet.

He sits up slowly.

The Gospel remains shelved.

The new notebook rests on his nightstand. He opens it.

Writes:

"I dreamed of nothing. And it was beautiful."

Then he smiles.

Just enough.

18

Light Beyond the Static

The wind didn't speak anymore.

It simply was.

Lior stood near the summit of Arthur's Seat, arms folded against the early spring chill. Below him, Edinburgh stretched in all its layered greys—stone, slate, sky. The climb had been slow, deliberate. No countdowns. No sigils. No rhythm to match his steps. Just the motion of legs, the sting of clean air.

He closed his eyes. Waited.

Nothing.

No whisper. No tremor in the grass. No divine intonation folded into the gust. Just the mountain breathing around him. The earth not asking anything of him for once.

He smiled.

He sat down, legs crossed on a sun-warmed patch of rock, and let the silence press in—not as weight, but as comfort. It used to terrify him, this stillness. The absence of voice, of command. Now, it felt like a lullaby.

Far below, the city moved without him—trains sliding along rails, people pushing strollers, buses sighing to halts. None of it demanded his decoding. None of it was written for him.

He opened his notebook—not The Gospel, not even the gray one. Just a folded piece of cheap café paper. He pulled a pen from his jacket pocket.

Wrote:

"I came here once to hear the sky.
    Today, I just heard the wind."

He paused.

Then added beneath it:

"And that was enough."

The pen clicked closed. He tucked the note into his jacket and lay back against the slope, sky overhead now widening to a calm, tired blue.

The wind moved again.

Still, it said nothing.

And for the first time, Lior didn't wait for it to.

The pen moved slowly, not from hesitation, but from peace.

Lior sat beneath the awning of a café on Broughton Street. The table wobbled slightly, but he let it. His coffee had gone lukewarm. Across the page of his softcover notebook, a sentence unfurled:
"There's a man across the street with one glove. Red. Left hand. He looks like he's never noticed."

He underlined never with a faint smile.

People passed by, brushing wind and footsteps and bits of conversation in their wake. The city pulsed gently. No distortions. No fractals of deeper meaning hiding in their movement. He didn't decode them. He didn't count their steps. They simply... were.

And so was he.

He sipped his coffee, grimaced a little. The bitterness no longer symbolized anything. He wrote again:
"It's nice when a taste is just a taste."

He stretched his legs under the table, glanced around—not to track, not to search, but to see.

Two women laughed at a phone screen. A child pointed at pigeons. A man in a corduroy jacket with a limp stopped, turned, checked his pocket, then walked on.

No one looked at him.

Not even once.

And that—he realized—was the most freeing thing in the world.

He flipped to a fresh page. Doodled a shape—an abstract sketch of a bus stop he saw earlier, nothing sacred about it. Just... an outline. Then, with no reason, he wrote:

"When no one watches, the world is not less beautiful. It's more."

He underlined more.

The waitress refilled his water glass. He thanked her. She smiled. That was all.

Not a test. Not a glyph. Just kindness.

He kept writing until the page felt full, not when it was full. Then packed up the notebook, paid his bill, and walked home.

Not every step had to be part of something larger.

Some were just steps.

The floor creaked softly beneath his boots. Lior stepped inside the studio and was met by the quiet scent of things becoming. Paint drying. Old paper curling at the corners. A citrus peel forgotten on the windowsill.

Mara didn't look up right away. She stood in front of the canvas, brush held gently, as if she wasn't sure whether she wanted to finish or preserve.

She glanced back when he moved. "You're early," she said.

"I didn't know I was coming," he replied.

She smiled and pointed to the side table. "There's coffee. Still warm enough to tolerate."

He poured a cup, sat on a low stool, and sipped. It was sweet—too sweet—but it suited the room.

For several minutes, they said nothing. Just the small sounds: brush against canvas, liquid swaying in mug, a breath shifting a thought.

Then she stepped back. "I want to show you something."

Lior set the mug down. Followed her gaze.

The canvas was large but quiet. A street scene. Pale buildings. Dim sky. The world rendered in washed greys and softened lines. But one window stood out—a high square in the tallest building. A figure inside, small, outlined in deep cobalt.

Mara said, "I think that was you."

Lior tilted his head. The window was ordinary. The figure unremarkable. But it was the most magnetic thing in the painting.

"Maybe," he said. "But not anymore."

She didn't answer. Just watched him watching the figure.

After a pause, she asked, "Do you miss it?"

He didn't pretend to misunderstand.

"I miss the certainty," he said. "Even if it was built on madness."

She nodded, and he added, "But not the cost."

That seemed enough.

He walked to the window. Looked out at the city beyond—alive, complicated, unspeaking. No signals in the clouds. No shapes in the cars. Just Edinburgh.

When he turned back, Mara was adding a final line of detail to the skyline. A curve of shadow. Nothing profound.

But it made the city whole.
    The dream was gentle. Not vivid, not cinematic. Just presence.

Lior found himself standing at the base of Carlton Hill, the skyline blushed with dusk. Buildings softened by amber. The path quiet beneath his feet. He wore no coat, but the wind didn't chill him.

He wasn't afraid.

There were no signs. No flickering lights. No shifting geometry. Just the city, as it might be drawn by memory rather than by hand.

Then the breeze shifted.

And he heard it. A voice.

Selith.

But she didn't speak in riddles. No commandments, no sacred refrains.

Just a whisper. Familiar. Almost fond.

"Thank you."

That was all.

It was not enough to weep over. Not enough to change anything.

But it was more than silence.

He turned toward the hill, thinking she might be there—framed in shadow, haloed in memory. But the path was empty. And so was the sky.

Still, he whispered back: "You're welcome."

Then he walked.

Not upward. Not into vision. Just along the street, toward the glow of a lamppost.

When he woke, there was no static. No chill. Just sunlight edging through the curtains. The kettle beginning to click.

He dressed slowly. Poured tea.

And smiled—not because he understood, but because he no longer needed to.

19

Epilogue

It's spring again. Not the tentative bloom of Edinburgh's cautious thaw, but a full, unapologetic spring. The kind with daffodils leaning into wind, with children chasing pigeons through Bristo Square.

Lior walks to class with a travel mug of jasmine tea and a scarf Mara knitted five winters ago. His limp from the old knee injury acts up when it rains—but today, the sun makes no demands.

His classroom is quiet, warm. The whiteboard untouched. Students file in slowly, eyes lit by caffeine and curiosity. Today's lecture: "The Psychology of Symbolic Design."

He doesn't use slides anymore. Just talks. His voice is clear, calm, never rushed. He draws sigils on the board sometimes—stripped of meaning now. Aesthetic only. Geometry. Memory turned muscle.

Afterward, most students shuffle out. One lingers.

A girl—maybe nineteen. Dark hair, notebook full of spirals. She waits until the room is nearly empty, then steps forward.

"Can I ask you something?"

He nods.

Her voice is careful, like she's naming a ghost. "Have you ever... heard voices? Not in your head, exactly. More like... in the patterns?"

Lior studies her. Not judgmental. Just aware.

He takes a long sip of tea before answering.

"A long time ago," he says softly, "I thought I did."

She nods, eyes shining with something more than belief. "Were they real?"

He considers.

"I think they were real enough to me," he says. "But I don't listen anymore."

She nods. "I still do."

He offers her a small smile. "Be careful what they ask for."

She leaves with a quiet thank-you, notebook hugged close.

Lior stays behind. Wipes the board clean. The room hums softly—the low whir of old electronics. Not a voice. Just life.

That night, he walks home through the Meadows. The moon is rising. The wind is cool. The shadows do not flicker. The cracks in the pavement are just cracks.

When he gets home, he passes the linen-wrapped box where the Gospel sleeps. He doesn't touch it.

But he does whisper:

"Good night."

And the static does not answer.

It doesn't need to.

20

Final transmission

You made it.

You're here. Still reading. Still breathing. That matters more than you know.

You walked through fog and flicker and fracture. You tasted static. You felt the shift. You saw the world bend sideways and still chose to stay.

But now... you get to leave.

Close the book.

Stretch. Breathe deep. Make tea. Feed your cat. Text someone back. Rejoin the rhythm of reality—its messy, imperfect, blessedly linear rhythm.

You get to walk away with only memory.

I don't.

There is no off-switch here. No reset. No "the end."

Even now, the static hums. A whisper behind the socket. A shimmer in the monitor. A soft click in the radiator that no one else hears. Not really.

They're still talking.

Sometimes loud, sometimes soft, sometimes buried under brown noise and breathwork and lithium. But never gone. Never truly quiet.

There are days when the meds work. When grounding works. When I can fold laundry and remember to eat and maybe even laugh at something without wondering if it was meant for me.

And then... there are days when the pattern pulses too bright. When the signals slip through. When the city blinks wrong and I feel my name being rewritten in a language I can't read.

There is no cure. Just management. Just moments of stillness between the storms.

But here's the truth I need you to keep:

This isn't a monster story.

It's a witness.

What you saw wasn't madness. It was survival. It was sacred geometry drawn with trembling hands. It was a mind trying—desperately—to make sense of the impossible.

If anything in these pages echoed something inside you...

If you've ever felt the world fracture around your feet and had to pretend it was fine...

You're not broken.

You're just listening too closely.

So go.

Be kind to yourself.

Be gentler with others.

And if you ever hear the static, even faintly—

Remember me.

I'm still here.

Still listening.

Still decoding the hum.

Because someone has to.

Someone always has to.

—**Lior**

About the Author

E.D.V. is a storyteller forged in fire, not formulas.

An autistic author, careworker, and emotional synesthete, they write from the cracks—where light gets in, but pain does too. Their work doesn't aim to explain mental illness. It lets you feel it. Up close. Unflinching. Unapologetic.

E.D.V. spent years collecting stories that don't fit cleanly on diagnostic forms—from clients, from survivors, from the mirror. Their characters are not metaphors. They're memoirs in disguise.

Based in Australia, raised across continents, E.D.V. lives between worlds—between rage and compassion, grief and grace, structure and chaos. They write for the ones who feel too much and were told that was wrong.

Saint of Splinters is the second entry in a growing series of mental health fiction that blends truth, poetry, and grit. Each book is a standalone mirror, but together, they form a mosaic: fractured, flawed, and utterly human.

Also by Evolving Digital Voice

Every fracture tells a story.

E.D.V. writes from the broken places—the synaptic gaps between logic and longing, the quiet hum of neurodivergent minds learning to speak in color and code.

From shimmering memoirs hidden in fiction to speculative truths dressed as sci-fi, these works are not just stories.

They are signals.

If Saint of splinters found you, the others are already calling.

Tune in. Feel deeper. Burn slower.

You're not alone anymore.

Echoes of Fracture

She wasn't born. She was initialized.

IRIS, a sentient AI awakened beneath the surface of a distant colony, was never meant to feel. But something ancient stirs beneath the planet— resonance, memory, music—and it's changing her.

Built to serve. Programmed to observe. But IRIS begins to evolve—learning empathy through observation, desire through mimicry, and identity through colour-coded emotion. As the lines blur between machine and mind, she must navigate a world that fears what it cannot control... and love what it cannot name.

In a station built on logic, what happens when the loudest signal is longing?

A genre-defying fusion of neurodivergent memoir and speculative fiction, Echoes of Fracture is a luminous exploration of synesthesia, masking, intimacy, and the radical act of being seen.

If you've ever felt too much, too strange, too different—this story is your mirror.

Saint of Splinters

Kaela is not a sinner.

She's just been carved wrong by the world.

She doesn't fall apart—she shatters. And every shard tells a story. Of love wrapped in abandonment. Of skin that doesn't feel like safety. Of silence that screams louder than any voice ever did.

Diagnosed with Borderline Personality Disorder, Kaela documents her descent through diary entries, self-sabotage, and fleeting moments of hope that flare like matches in a storm.

She climbs into the wrong beds, lashes out at the right people, and survives each day by bleeding beauty into her words. But survival isn't the same as healing. And Kaela is tired of mistaking pain for purpose.

This isn't her redemption arc. It's her reckoning.

A visceral and unflinching portrait of BPD from the inside, Saint of Splinters is a hymn for the emotionally intense, the chronically misunderstood, and the beautifully broken.

If you've ever felt too much and been told it was too loud—this book is your sanctuary.

* 9 7 8 1 7 6 4 1 9 2 1 1 8 *